PS
3558
.A 65
S4

Harrington

Secret swinger

Also by Alan Harrington

Life in the Crystal Palace (1959)
The Revelations of Dr. Modesto (1955)

*These are Borzoi Books,
published in New York by Alfred A. Knopf*

THE SECRET SWINGER

1 9 6 6

THE SECRET SWINGER

by ALAN HARRINGTON

New York: Alfred · A · Knopf

L. C. catalog card number: 66-12393

THIS IS A BORZOI BOOK,

PUBLISHED BY ALFRED A. KNOPF, INC.

First Edition

To Steve and Virginia,
and to John and Shirley Holmes

Now there are times when a whole generation
is caught . . . between two ages, between two
modes of life and thus loses the feeling
for itself, for the self-evident, for all
morals, for being safe and innocent.

—HERMANN HESSE
Steppenwolf

Contents

(ix

CONTENTS

PART III: *Nowhere*

PART IV: *The Search*

PART I « *The Bar* »

« 1 »

At Shannon's

ON MOST WORKING DAYS George Pectin had drinks and lunch at Shannon's, a Manhattan sporting bar favored by magazine and book publishing people. At noon a dozen *Forecast* staff men might be found there. Shannon's was convenient and had become a sort of club with traditions, unwritten laws, and comforting taboos. For example, you could be as noisy and even quarrelsome as you pleased at the bar. You would *never* disturb anyone who chose to drink by himself at one of the shadowy corner tables.

(3

Every table at Shannon's was covered with a red-and-white-checkered cloth. The cobwebbed walls were hung with photographs, some enthusiastically inscribed to Jim Shannon, of long lost actors, fighters, and jockeys. "Jim!" the owner of one vaguely handsome face had scrawled. "I'll never forget how you boosted me up the ladder!" What ladder? Who? This message was signed by Austin Smythe.??? An early joke among the habitués of Shannon's concerned the obscurity of the hopefuls along the wall. From this mockery developed the humorous custom of ransacking old shops to find new candidates for anonymity. As each faded hope was brought in, it was placed in an alcove, where it remained for a year. If no one could identify the figure in the photograph, it was placed in the "Hall of Oblivion." But it was never doomed. Should the actor or athlete be plucked out of nowhere and (after a long, pleasing wrangle) positively identified by some new drinker at the bar, out went the photograph. Thus, at Shannon's, even obscurity was not quite permanent.

Women could be served at Shannon's but were seldom brought there, and felt out of place. The floor was covered with sawdust. Warm and softly lit, the big room smelled of hamburgers and onions. Faint sounds of tape-recorded jazz came from speakers on either side of a great oval mirror. The bar itself was beautiful, of shining mahogany. Its altar of glowing bottles rose nearly to the ceiling.

A dozen years before, when George Pectin began coming to Shannon's, two young fellows from Ireland had taken over the bar. They had aged with breath-taking swiftness, growing jowls, turning gray and then white at more than ten times the aging rate of their patrons. One had just died.

George Pectin, coming in out of the cold rain mixed with sleet, stamped on the welcome mat. He was a slender, youngish man with dark circles under his eyes.

"Some weather, Mr. Pectin." A somber, courteous face greeted him from behind the cash register.

"You're not kidding, Vito."

At the far end of the bar the surviving Irish boy bowed, as though hanged. George moved to his accustomed place, the last stool near the door. The new man awaited his pleasure with folded arms.

"What'll it be?" he said jovially.

"Vodka. Rocks. Bitters."

George glanced at the new man. Thin, amiable, scruffy, could use a haircut. He wasn't much for talking with barmen, cab drivers, and the like.

"There you are, sir. Of course, it's not the best medicine in the world for those bags!"

Please, not another harpoon. The new man stood with his arms folded, chuckling. In my present state, thought George Pectin, I seem to be a target for everybody. Lately people had been casting all kinds of ego-diminishing missiles at him. After each one he felt a little less sure of himself. Why did they do this? Perhaps it was a matter of aesthetics. Certain faces asked to be punched. So too, the solitary drinker decided, the man who has lost his way invites unsettling remarks from others.

He was forty-three years old and had lost his way. The brief walk from the *Forecast* Building to Shannon's made him miserably cold. Curtains of rain were sweeping and drifting across the city. Rain beat on the roofs of the corner newspaper stands, rattled on taut awnings, and sprayed the glass office buildings. Haze moved loosely through the streets. He could see the tops of the skyscrapers, and then they were gone.

On a day like this Shannon's was more than ever a refuge. He heard familiar sounds. The regulars were coming. Gathering drinkers stamped in, shedding their coats, kicking off their overshoes. Some wore plastic hat covers. There was more stamping. Gazing into his drink, George was aware of a nervous presence at the bar.

"God damn, Vito, how are you?"

"Fine, Mr. Rhodes," answered the manager. He rubbed his hands and called out to the new bartender: "Virginia Gentleman on the rocks!"

"Giving away my secrets again, Vito!"

Vito: "Ha, ha, ha!" He had grown used to the individual ways of the gentlemen from *Forecast* and the publishing houses. They had made his place fashionable—so much so that famous artists and cartoonists in various stages of drunkenness had been pleased to create obscene drawings on the white walls of the cellar. You were taken to see them, as a sign of being in at Shannon's. Philip Rhodes, *Forecast*'s second-string editorial writer, had been in for years.

"Vito," he said, sliding onto his favorite stool. "Do you know who I despise?"

"No, Mr. Rhodes— Good afternoon, gents. The bar? No? ..."

"Phony liberals, that's who."

"I'm against phonies too, Mr. Rhodes," said Vito, gradually moving away to seat the newcomers.

"Naturally you are. And of all the phonies, the phony liberal is the worst—and that goes for you, George Pectin!"

It was a game. George smiled and waved at the familiar insult, which for this stage of the afternoon (12:05) was mild and friendly. Within a few minutes a host of soft men would be gathered about the bar begging for Bloody Marys, and Phil Rhodes would almost certainly become embroiled with someone.

The voice of *Forecast*'s enlightened conservatism came from a small man in his late forties, nearly bald, with protruding blue eyes. An amazing thing about him was the contrast between his immense bass voice and his extraordinarily narrow shoulders. He had simply been forgotten when it came to shoulders, and the pads inserted by his tailor bobbed like epaulets.

"Phil!"

"Hi there, Jimbo!"

Carrying a fresh drink, George Pectin moved to a corner table in the shadows. Gloomily he watched the opinion-formers gather. The smells of wet sawdust and overshoes mingled with those of hamburger, onions, and the breath of whisky. He made a sign to Joey, the old waiter, indicating another drink and his usual cheeseburger from the grill.

He dwelt on the painful events that had depressed him. They had been instructive, but he was tired of learning. At forty-three a man should have earned the right to take on a little complacency, like fat. This right had been denied him. (He remained skinny too. Liquor fatigued his system and drew circles under his eyes, but would not fatten him up.)

It's a bad idea, taking stock, he thought. You always end up with a lower opinion of yourself. Even so, it was time to turn his life around. The glowing bottles in back of Shannon's bar gave him a churchly feeling. This was an atheist's church. Racks of wine bottles presented a battery of corks, and the effect was that of an organ. With the murmuring jazz in counterpoint, the wine-bottle organ picked up the themes that had been troubling him.

« 2 »

George Pectin Before the Bar

HE IMAGINED THE COSMOS around him taking the form of an enormous wheel. One man's experience was a smaller wheel. The century, the times, his awareness of life, turned on a central axis. George refrained from using this image pretentiously, and didn't build a philosophy on it. The wheel simply appeared in his thoughts when he reflected to any depth.

The image also came mixed, and occurred to him in several dimensions. There was the well-known Wheel of

Time. It surrounded the world, turning more quickly in small towns, particularly the town you grew up in. One fled to New York to avoid aging, noticeable time. In Manhattan, where a man scrambled for free hours, it had become possible, strangely enough, to make time almost stand still until one suddenly died—because New York (forget Boston) was now the hub of the universe, and the turn of each year didn't make too much difference in East Midtown.

There was in George's view the Career Wheel. He visualized the struggle to "make it in New York" in terms of a flat, spinning wheel at Coney Island. Paying your money, you made for the center of the disk, which slowly began to spin. As the centrifugal force increased, you clung for a hand hold, groping for the hub. But if you didn't find a niche, you were eventually flung out to the perimeter and off, back to the sticks where you came from.

A man was broken on the wheel, or became one. This was all part of a master design, George Pectin tried to believe. Each of us must be "spinning somewhere." All things were contained by a rim, ultimately made sense, and moved in a mysteriously right path. Justice usually made itself felt. Quality, particularly one's own, would tell in the long run.

A memory came back to him now in Shannon's bar. He was on the front porch of his house, in Boston, six years old. His mother knelt before him, tying his necktie, saying: "You are a member of the upper middle class." Was not his grandfather, the Scotsman, a member of The Country

Club in Brookline? And his other grandfather, dead earlier in the century, secretary of the St. Botolph Club and a former dean of the Harvard Law School? "You have the right stuff in you," she said, tucking in his shirt tail.

Another memory joined this one. It was much more recent. He was getting married in the afternoon. Somebody said his father had arrived. Arthur Pectin sat down with a strange, bright eagerness. To his astonishment, George saw that this time there wouldn't be commonplaces. His father was bending toward him earnestly.

"You see, nobody ever told me what to do, George. I got out of college, and didn't know how to begin." Watching his son pull at the lapels of the cutaway, he went on: "Finally I got a job in Chicopee, in a machine shop. All I did was just hang around. Nobody bothered to teach me. Then there was the cotton mill in Fall River. You know, start from the ground up. The foreman resented me. I guess he thought I was a smart-alecky college boy. But I wasn't a smart aleck at all. I only wanted to know what to do, and it was that way with every job. When I married your mother, and your grandfather made me agency director, selling insurance, for which I wasn't fitted, and knew it," his father cried out, "you don't know how I'd get up every morning with *wildcats in my stomach*."

Friday nights came at last with a groan of relief, Mah Jong, martinis rattling in the silver shaker. He remembered at twilight the footsteps coming up the front walk and his father's faint song:

There are no bones in ice cream
Hello, hello, hello!

Arthur Pectin's hands trembled on top of an ivory-headed cane. He cast shy, boyish glances around. The bridegroom eyed his father curiously and wondered: Why is he confiding in me now?

YEARS LATER he stirred his drink at Shannon's and asked himself whether his own problem wasn't one of genetic fatigue. Conceivably the ancestral blood had thinned. Could genes fade or become flaccid? But that was hardly fair. His father had suffered a streptococcus infection in his teens, and had to stay in a wheel chair for a year. The habit of dependency might have dated from that time. Also he was a skilled artisan, made beautiful ship models, trays, and lamps. The circumstance that his craft was not needed at this point in history had nothing to do with blood being thin.

Even so, this failure to adapt which I seem to have inherited from him, George Pectin thought, may be part of a larger natural selection in which my kind of person is going to be filtered out. Look at our marriage, a union of weak respiratory systems; my sinusitis and Mary's collapsed lung and Darwinian TB. Davey is healthy enough, yes, but we had luck there.

He reminded himself of the years before Mary's illness. The young couple had somehow lacked drive, a sense of reality. Reconciled to being childless, they drifted through a complacent and shabby youth. Then, late in their thirties, against all the doctors' predictions, the baby had come. His birth had taken thirty-three hours. As it turned out, Mary never fully recovered, and four years later her health gave way completely.

All that was over. With her year in the sanatorium coming to an end, she looked forward cheerfully to a new start. But in her absence he had painfully rediscovered himself, and made a resolution. He was determined to avoid a genteel Anglo-Saxon middle age. In a few weeks there would be no way to get around telling her: I'm not coming back.

One day a note arrived from his grandfather. It had no special purpose except to remark: "Glad to hear you're doing well on that magazine," and to inveigh against his ailing legs: "I used to be an athlete, but now I am ashamed." The old man—no longer magnificent, but still, even blurry-eyed and eighty-seven, George Pectin's final judge on earth—had abruptly concluded: "Old age strikes a man like thunder, Your Loving Grandad."

Now forty-three had struck for him, more like a warning bell. Get going, time is short. Warning flags were up all over the course. No more promises. Nearly everybody he knew had surpassed him, leaving the obscure staff reporter behind. The wild and rebellious, seemingly impractical friends he had knocked about with in his Greenwich Village days had become famous. Other stodgy ones with less ability had persisted and somehow made reputations. He had moved indecisively in neutral ground between the rebellious and the stodgy.

It's not too late, he said to the bright bottles. I'm still young enough to break my pattern.

"Joey, another vodka!"

FOR A YEAR he had trudged up the hillside road to the sanatorium. There his wife lay with her rare infection complicated by TB. The disease resisted, falling back little by little as they shot new antibiotics into her. Mary Pectin waited for his visit every fortnight.

Motionless clouds lowered on the hills. He walked up to this sky along a winding black-top road. The afternoon was silent; the calm sky soundproofed everything. White birches hung motionless, looking down at him like a cluster of old men. Along the way he passed pure snow patches and spoiled a number of them with his footprints. He welcomed the dog who charged from the farmhouse and barked alongside him. He came to the chicken farm and the pony in the field to whom he fed sugar. The pony trotted to the wire fence shaking his head and snorting happily, and nosed over the two lumps he held out. George loved to feel the pony's mane and the muzzle of prickly velvet.

He headed for the snow-white sanatorium on top of the hill. Even now, he thought, she's probably got me zeroed in from one of the windows, following every move I make.

Mary grew prettier with his every visit. This afternoon

her plump and rosy cheeks surprised him. He observed for the first time that she had gained back practically all of her lost weight. Now, leaning on his arm during the hour they were permitted in the social room, she whispered: "Dr. Ralston thinks I'll be able to come home *before* spring!"

He said uneasily: "Are you sure?"

"Oh, yes, if Ralston says so."

She went on talking about Davey, and how he was getting along with his aunt and uncle in Tennessee. "He writes the most understanding letters for a little boy. Of course, he dictates them to Janet. You have the kindest sister."

They were silent, and she said with tears in her eyes: "After a year, do you think he'll recognize me?"

"Naturally he will. He has your picture by his bed table."

"Haven't I changed?"

"No."

"I *haven't*?"

"You look . . . much better."

They looked out on the winter-barren garden and the white marble dryad about to dance. She touched his hand, and he did his best to respond. But he was wondering: Can I tell her yet? No, she might have a relapse.

"Poor dear, you're tired. That miserable train ride . . ."

It was the marriage state itself that would be unbearable. There would be nothing new. Cheerful, utterly pat celebrations of Christmas morning, birthdays, anniversaries, and the birth of children would once again send him into fits of gloomy dissent. Amid terrible harmlessness, the years would wheel swiftly by. He could imagine her thinking: We'll grow old together. But he didn't want to age with anybody. In his year of being alone he had learned to frug and do the Monkey. At parties young people treated him as one of them.

She would have to settle down with Davey somewhere, perhaps near her family in Connecticut. Not that he would abandon them. On the contrary, after the divorce he would probably become more attentive. Visit every week . . .

"Aunt May was here. She brought me a Christmas basket and sent Davey *The Bible in Pictures*."

"Rushing the season a bit."

"She always does."

It was half-past three in the dark afternoon. Two hours would pass before he would be on the train back to New York.

"That kind of present isn't exactly what a little boy is hoping for, but how would Aunt May know?"

The virtues of irreproachable Christian womanhood turned to him. But she wasn't prissy. She opened her light-blue quilted gown a little. He became aware of the light lavender scent she had put on for him. The open sensuality in her gentle young-mother's face embarrassed him.

"Excuse me, dear."

He saw the stethoscope and the doctor beckoning. Mary's stately walk to the door took a full minute. He noticed that all of the convalescing women moved in the same way. The social room resembled a harbor on a calm afternoon. The patients bore themselves proudly—their ambulatory hour had been earned after months in bed, day and night, lying out on the cold porches.

"Mary, I won't . . ."

"What, darling?"

"I'm not going back to another drab apartment. . . ."

She looked at him in bewilderment. "But it won't be that way."

"Yes, it will!"

"I'll do much better this time. You'll see."

"*You can't.* I mean, your condition. You won't be able to keep house. The dust . . ."

"I don't see why not. What was wrong with our little house?"

"Shabby genteel! Doomed. . . . No! I won't go back to *dust!*" he cried. "That's why I took my 'clean, airy room for business gentleman' and put your things in storage. I had to *clear out.* Get away from slanting parquet floors, traffic noise, exhaust fumes coming in through the window. . . ."

"But how could I—?"

"Threads of dust on the walls; the thrift-shop rug saturated with dust that can't be swept, vacuumed, or beaten out of it. Dust on your smock, on the books and records, and—"

"Was it my fault that we hadn't the money?" she said with quiet indignation.

"We had enough," he said, "to do more than we did, with what we had. Oh, it's not just your fault. Mine too. I'm not blaming you, dear. . . ." He looked down in embarrassment.

"What is it that you want to tell me, George?"

He continued to look at the floor. "I don't know. I just wanted to—make things clear," he said. "I *am* tired. Don't feel well."

He made a gesture toward comforting her, and stood up. "See you in two weeks!"

« *3* »

Gretchen in Yorkville

His cheeseburger was ballast for him in the sea of vodka; insurance that he wouldn't tip over or get off course amid his memories and ram into icebergs, cutting his forehead as he once did.

As if it were Saturday night, he heard the voice again.

"Pectin!"

At Grand Central he had taken a cab to the cocktail party, arriving late. As he came in the door, he saw that the party was reaching its climax. The din around him reverberated into a kind of silence. He couldn't hear anybody, or move, it seemed, in any direction to seek out a face, and if he had he wouldn't know what to say to that face. Heads bobbed everywhere around. Glasses clinked. Every now and then hands reached past him into a bowl of potato chips.

He sensed a flurry of movement near the window. A man came pushing through the crowd, using his elbows. He had a glazed, shocked look. Obviously a glass of liquor had been flung at his head. His cheekbone was wet, and whisky dribbled from his shoulder down to the jacket pocket. The incident produced a moment of quiet, and once more George's name was called.

He hadn't heard this voice for two years.

"Gretchen," he said to the dark, heavy girl with black hair falling to her shoulders. "How are you . . ."

"Get me a drink." She spoke with the usual mocking intonation, and her bold eyes found him as amusing as ever.

She sat with her bottom on the arm of the couch. An indignant girl was trying to rub stains from her dress, and several guests were hunting for ice cubes on the rug.

"It was you," he said, taking the wet glass from her.

". . . a ridiculous man."

In the kitchen, where the bar was, he mixed a scotch and water. He turned to find her at his shoulder.

"You're nervous, Pectin. What are you doing?"

"Now?" he asked.

"Of course, now."

"I ought to . . ." He hesitated. When Gretchen was in

this mood, he knew, they would end up in the German bars and dance halls between Third and Second Avenue in Yorkville. Painful memories came back. He didn't want anything more to do with the strange game she had liked to play with him.

"I'm going," Gretchen said. "Do you want to take me out?"

AT THE BREW HOUSE on East Fifty-fourth Street they dined on rare roast beef with an enormous baked potato. The dinner made her pensive for a time, but they drank wine too. She became sleepy, then suddenly wide awake, and at ten o'clock when they emerged she was ready for the town.

Gretchen linked her exciting, fat arm in his and they caught a taxi. Now he tried his best as always to persuade himself that he didn't care what happened. Become a spectator; it was the only way.

At the first German bar he remembered that he hadn't made his regular Saturday-evening phone call to Davey in Tennessee.

"Oh, hell, I hope he hasn't gone to bed."

"You are a dear father," said Gretchen. "Please don't leave me too long or I'll get involved in something."

In the booth he made his long-distance connection, and watched her through the glass. She could lean at a forty-five-degree angle from a bar stool and, as drunk as she might be, never come near falling over. She had a full mouth and widely spaced arrogant gray eyes. She gazed around the bar in a manner he knew very well, with a comic, rather evil expression, and the men were instantly watchful as she stared at each of them in turn.

"New York calling."

"Yes!"

"Hi, Davey."

"Dad!"

"How are you?"

"I'm fine. Guess what."

Their conversation seldom amounted to much, but usually there was a detail.

"Uncle Jim took us to the top of a mountain where it was all snow, and we slid down on flying saucers."

"That sounds wonderful."

"Yes."

When his sister came on, George asked: "How is he?"

"Well . . . all right. But with five in the house, it is a bit trying. I don't suppose you can do anything."

"Janet, you know how we appreciate this. If you can just hang on another few months. Mary *is* getting better."

"Oh, we'll hang on. There's nothing else to do. You needn't worry about him. But I do want you to know that as soon as you're able . . . Here he is."

"Goodbye, Dad. I miss you."

"Goodbye, Davey. See you soon."

"And Mummy too?"

"Very soon."

For once Gretchen wasn't involved. She had pushed the

button for a German rock 'n' roll song on the jukebox, and was peacefully swaying to the rhythm. They sat for hours in the bar, and he lost track of time. At one point she took his hand in a comradely way and winked at him. Now that I've made up my mind not to get involved with her, he thought, she's wonderfully easy to be with. She hadn't been so when it mattered. The evenings he had tried to steal with her had been filled with shocks.

Gretchen had a beautiful contralto voice and spoke in Eastern boarding school accents. At one bar in the course of an early date he had been disturbed to hear this voice interrupted by the question:

"Watcha doon these days, Gwetchen?"

Looking up anxiously, he had beheld on the other side of his date a flashy hoodlum.

"Hi ya," he said to George. His eyes darted cold amusement from under the panama hat. He was bronzed and wore white on white, and a pale-gray tie, and might have stepped off the plane from Miami. "Hey, wea you been, Gwetchen? How come I don't see you no more?"

"Oh, Vincent, why do you always sneak up on me? You're such a pill."

The man had winked at George. "Fresh, ain't she? You ought to see heh bedwoom, hey Gwetchen. All those books and wecords. Tell me some more of that Shakespeare, Gwetchen, that you told me befow."

"Oh, Vincent," she said, leaning drunkenly away and regarding him like a lady owl, "won't you ever tell me what you do for a living?"

"Like I said, I couldn't tell you, Gwetchen. Suppose I was with the FBI now. Would I tell you?"

Vincent strolled off, and the watcher, chilled by his date's familiarity with this person, asked in a small voice: "You know him?"

"I woke up with him. After that it was sort of a habit."

That night he had taken her home with enormous expectations. She had crumpled on her bed murmuring: "I'd like to sleep with you." Her lighted cigarette fell from her fingers onto the blue sheet, and he rescued it.

"That's nice. Is there someone here who wants some beer?"

To his dismay he realized that she was talking to any man. She lay in full-blown disorderly beauty, drunk and helpless, not knowing his name or her own, her dress crushed and hiked up, revealing her fabulous white thighs moving softly together. He remained transfixed by the softly moving power of these legs, Gretchen's great hips, and as she moaned and moved in her drunken sleep, he felt intimidated by the cavernous sensuality displayed before him. It seemed to be awaiting an enormous climax that every experience she had ever known would contribute to.

George Pectin knew that all he had to do was ease off her slip, and . . . It hadn't seemed quite right to make love to a woman in this state. He would have to go home; she'd wake up with a headache and not even remember who had been with her. There would be other times. He hid her cigarettes so that she wouldn't set herself on fire, tucked her into the blue sheets, and left.

It was the last chance he had. Thereafter she had teased and put him off, taunting him about Mary being left at home ("Patient Griselda"), petted him ("You have a nice body"), denounced him ("You have the least physical presence of any man I have ever known; you project nothing"), admired him ("You are brilliant sometimes"), pitied him ("You are in hell"), and denied him ("As I get closer to the bed, my interest in you dies").

After a while he understood that he had been singled out for an infuriating distinction. She who must have gone to bed with three hundred men refused him—and took special pleasure in doing so. Then he had sensibly given up. He ran into her occasionally, each time with a different man, twice with her Peruvian lover, who lasted considerably longer than the others. Evidently he too was gone. So was the man just now, with the drink thrown in his face. So were all her old suitors, those who had made it and the few who hadn't; the playboys and taxi drivers, a United States senator, Latin American diplomats, television repair men, poets and house painters, the tennis pro, ski instructors, longshoremen, the stockbroker she had married and immediately divorced, hoodlums and shoe clerks, had visited her and passed on, and there would be many more before she quit. Gretchen was in mid-career, a little fatter and coarser than a few years ago, becoming immense but still beautifully solid. The men would come and go for years yet, except for the abiding one, her father, who had laughed when he called her a whore and once bit her lip when he kissed her.

In her bedroom at two in the morning, Gretchen, choking with sobs, opened her Bible and read from the Gospel of Luke: "Daughters of Jerusalem, weep not for me, but weep for yourselves, and for your children. For, behold, the days are coming, in which they will say, 'Blessed are the barren, and the wombs that never bore, and the paps which never gave suck . . . !' "

"WHAT ARE YOU mooning about, Pectin?"

"I was thinking of you."

"It won't do you any good."

"I'm aware of that, Gretchen."

"Come on!" she said. "Don't be so gloomy." Swinging off the bar stool, she looked at him maliciously and said: "There's a place I want to go to. The singer with the band. I love him. If you'd rather not come with me, you can go home."

It was past midnight. Although he knew it was silly, he felt responsible for her.

"All right," he said. "I'd just as soon come along, at least for a while."

The dance hall was on East Eighty-sixth Street near Second Avenue. The singer's name was Jo Boyne. He had black curly hair and dark eyes and a smooth, pale countenance. When he smiled, as he did for Gretchen, he put something mysterious into it. This made her feel, she explained to George Pectin, "as if he already knows me." They were not in fact acquainted, except that she had been

there the week before. Over the objections of a stuffy escort, she had invited him to the table. After a few minutes
he had been forced to excuse himself and get ready for the
final floor show. Then she had made numerous requests for
Rodgers and Hart songs, and he had sung "Bewitched" and
"My Funny Valentine" directly to her, doing it so obviously that the real estate man had become furious and
rushed her out. But not before she had exchanged signals
with Jo Boyne. Tonight. . . .

"My Funny Valentine!" sang Jo Boyne as the couples
swayed on the floor, and colored lights like bubbles played
among the chandeliers.

At the table Gretchen said: "Have you got twenty dollars?"

"What for?" George asked suspiciously.

The last time one of her written requests to Jo Boyne
had been wrapped around a twenty-dollar bill. George was
shocked.

"Gretchen, why do you do that? You don't have to.
You cheapen yourself."

"I want him."

"Well, I'm not going to give you twenty dollars for
that."

"Oh, crumb. Let's dance then. Dance by him."

They did, and Gretchen beckoned to the singer: "Come
to our table!"

Jo Boyne nodded, including George in his courteous
acceptance of the idea.

"East of the Sun, West of the Moon!"

"Isn't he terrif!" she said, as they went back to their table.

"He's very good-looking, but I think he whines a bit."

"You're jealous!" She shot a malevolent look at him.

"I'm not, Gretchen."

She glowered, but was evidently not in the mood to pick a fight. Instead a smile came to her lips, and she said: "When he comes, you can take lessons from him."

George yawned and said: "I hope he comes soon. I'm tired."

Gretchen leaned back and watched the colored bubbles swirl around the ceiling. It worried George to see that she was beginning to loll. Her mouth was half open and the expression on her face was at once sensual, cruel, and silly. Strands of hair waved about her cheeks and she had taken on the appearance of untidiness.

The music ended, and Jo Boyne's round, flawless face came before them. He pulled out a chair and sat down by Gretchen. He inclined toward her, and his head, the tumbling curls and knowing eyes, approached her bosom, and he smiled. Gretchen looked down at him over her bosom, and smiled lazily. She ran her fingers through his curls before he laughingly pulled away.

George Pectin ordered a round of drinks and they talked about Jo Boyne's career. He was soon to appear in Cincinnati. George nodded and looked openly at his watch, making it clear both to Gretchen and to Jo Boyne that he didn't care what they did. It was two-thirty—time on Sun-

day morning for the last dance. The singer pressed Gretch-
en's hand and thanked George. The musicians came back
to the bandstand for their last set.

George ordered a final round and said: "Probably I
ought to go. Is that what you want?"

"Do as you please!" she said angrily. "I'm going home
with him." Gretchen called out hoarsely: "I've Got a
Crush on You!"

Jo Boyne held the microphone tenderly and sang out
"My Blue Heaven!" Gretchen cried: "I've Got a Crush
on You!" and he sang "I've Got My Love to Keep Me
Warm."

While George was paying the check she commanded:
"Lend me twenty dollars until tomorrow. I'll pay you
tomorrow!"

"Gretchen!" he protested. "I haven't got it. See." He
showed his wallet.

The hall was emptying except for a few couples on the
floor lingering as Jo Boyne sang "Goodnight, Sweetheart."

"We're the last ones. Let's go," George said. When
Gretchen stood up he saw that she was quite drunk. Lip-
stick, a handkerchief, and cigarettes spilled from her purse
along with some change, and he picked up everything. She
left him kneeling by the table. George saw her approach Jo
Boyne, who was talking with the saxophonist at the bandstand.

Coming up to tender Gretchen her purse, he heard Jo
Boyne say: "I'm sorry. There must be some misapprehen-
sion on your part."

"You're coming home with me!"

"I beg your pardon." Contemptuous eyes and a smooth face looked down on her. "We're supposed to mingle with the customers, but at three o'clock I'm off duty."

She dragged at his arm: "Come on!"

Coldly Jo Boyne shrugged her from him, saying: "Please don't demean yourself. Try to think of the appearance you make. You are embarrassing your escort. For your information, I have a wife and four children who see little enough of me, and I'm going home now. We have to get up early for church. I suggest that you do the same."

IN THE TAXI she said: "You were jealous of him. Well, you can come up, but you can't have me. Just be sure of that."

"It's all right, Gretchen."

"You don't have to console me."

"I know."

"Don't be patronizing."

"I'm not, Gretchen. I'm just sorry."

"Oh, crumb!"

"I'll see you to the door. I'm tired."

"Well, that's a good idea, because you can't have me."

« 4 »

I Am as a Child

AT HOME THAT NIGHT he had found the notice of an undelivered telegram in the front hall. He walked to the all-night Western Union office on Lexington Avenue, and found that the telegram was from his uncle and announced the death of his grandmother: LAURIE DIED LAST NIGHT. FUNERAL MONDAY AFTERNOON TWO O'CLOCK. DOUGAL.

She was eighty-seven and had barely been aware of her surroundings for a number of years. The last time he visited she hadn't recognized him. Even so, as he walked down Lexington Avenue past dark drugstores and restaurants filled with upended chairs, he felt sorry and frightened that she could die.

From out of the night around him came a burst of laughter. It came from one of the black windows along the avenue, and a voice close to him inquired anxiously: "Are you all right, sir? Can I help you?"

"No," George Pectin replied, "it's just that I feel this sort of contemptuous voice, not yours but another one, sometimes a chorus of voices, following me around, seeming to be a commentary on me, laughing out loud at what I hold dear."

"They're only enjoying their drinks, sir. Are you all right?"

He looked up and saw an arm and a folded napkin, and the earnest face of Joey, the waiter at Shannon's. "Hey, Joey, you must think I'm a nut, talking to myself, but believe me I'm not drunk. It's not that. I'll have another vodka."

"Another cheeseburger, sir?"

"All right, Joey, another cheeseburger."

And another volley of laughter from the bar. He heard the new barman call out in his over-familiar way: "Here we are! What'll you have?" and the journalist answered: "Bloody Mary!"

Philip Rhodes was making his scene.

"You may be a native-born New Englander, but you don't know what you're talking about!"

The argument concerned the proper way to make a hot

buttered rum. *Forecast*'s editorial writer insisted that the final concoction ought to be mulled with a hot poker. The barman laughed and remarked that either way you would get just as drunk. A clamorous argument spread, involving a quartet of experts.

George Pectin had often wished that the readers of *Forecast* could have a chance to see these opinion-formers at noon. They would find it difficult to stand in awe of them. Yet, he thought, they are awe-inspiring in a way. It was a tribute to basic intelligence and guts that these men could put out a magazine at all. Many of the editors who supervised or wrote stories about heart transplants, underwater cities, and the astronauts' back-yard cook-outs were under the influence of liquor a good deal of the time. Including me, George admitted. I'm not a drunk but I do drink too much, and will have to cut down.

It was still possible to drink and get a job done by working in short bursts, in the early part of the day or late at night, deadlining with the collar torn open. While the cleaning women labored through fluorescent offices in skyscrapers all over the city, you could do it at the last minute, whacking it out, cutting it down, or pasting it up in silence, except for the pecking typewriters of a few other midnight workers, week after week. Will there come a week, George sometimes worried, when I won't be able to do it—like Larry and Frank? Then what? Patience and understanding from the magazine, of course; a rest. Intermittent comebacks, an end to forgiveness, and then?

(*33*

He wondered why alcohol flowed in the arteries of this great and successful publication. Its writers weren't the only ones who could be seen drinking Bloody Marys in the morning. On the business side as well you could find a high percentage of booze-fighters. There had been the scandalous sales meeting on the Caribbean island. On arrival at the airport there had been an unexpected delay. The visitors had been held in the plane for a while. Then the ladder was placed alongside the airliner. Local officials waited in vain for the Yankees to come smiling down the gangplank in their white linen suits. Nothing happened. It became necessary to go aboard and get them, to pour them from the plane, the wounded soldiers of enlightened capitalism. They slept it off, met again, conferred and argued and made decisions, but they also drank and fought; there was a frightening knee-and-fist battle between two key executives.

Not even the island whorehouses benefited from the visit of these strange men. They drank and lay out under the moon. How they hated to leave! One went so far as to lash himself to a palm tree. He had to be pried loose and escorted to the New York-bound plane by means of a judo hold.

THE SUNDAY AFTER HIS grandmother died he had spent most of the day walking around Central Park. Of course, he promised, I'll go to Cape Cod and look at her in the coffin. His grandfather, whom he loved, was the only person he dreaded seeing. He couldn't bear to watch the old man cry—as he almost certainly would after sixty-three years of marriage.

George climbed up the steps to the castle in Central Park near Seventy-second Street and looked out over the battlements to the playground where two schoolboy football teams struggled on the turf.

His grandfather, who now hobbled with a cane, had once been a rugby star in Montreal. The Scottish immigrant had proceeded to Toronto and met the girl who would be his fiancée. (He had known from the first moment in the garden that this was his life partner.) Did he propose marriage then? Not yet. Before taking such an important step he had to make his way in the world. After reaching an "understanding" with the beautiful Canadian girl, he went on down to Boston. There he briskly sold life insurance, saved his money, bought a house and painstakingly furnished it stick by stick, decorated it (putting up the window curtains himself), and only *then* did he march back up to Canada—two and one-half years later—and claim his bride.

I can never match his performance, mused George Pectin. To love the same woman for sixty-three years, never allow doubt into the marriage, never to think of leaving her somewhere along the way for a younger, more exciting woman!

Tomorrow the old man would break down and weep for

her. He might also be crying because *he* was eighty-seven years old and alone, and about to follow her into the ground—which he desperately didn't want to do.

His grandfather hadn't been a churchgoer or a philosophical man, preferring action, business, golf, cards, brandy and cigars. But two autumns before his eighty-seventh year—having acknowledged the night nurse and kissed his unconscious wife—he had hobbled to his writing desk. There he had penned out a letter: "To my children & their children & their children." This message stated:

> I believe there is a Creator of this World. There must be a Creator when you see the wonderful anatomy of All Human Beings & all Animals—all the fish —all birds and all the beautiful flowers that grow—all the Trees all the Crops that feed the Human Race.
>
> When the Creator made us all—then he has the Power to resurrect us after death. . . .
>
> I believe we live after death in our children & their children & they continue the load for us & live the good life.
>
> I am as a child.
>
> I don't know everything about Life. I don't know why we are here in this World but do know we live and die.
>
> Life is a Great Mystery & the Creator only knows. The American Indians had a religion of their own. They worshipped the Sun-Moon-Stars-Rivers-Mountain Lakes & Ocean & they believed in a Great Spirit.
>
> So my children look upon Life seriously you are only in this Life a short time   DAD

During George's last brief visit to Cape Cod, his grandfather had tapped his cane on the porch and ordered him: "Take your mother (!) for a walk!" Obediently he said: "Come on, Laurie," and took his grandmother's arm. They moved a few inches at a time along the sidewalk. He made conversation, saying practically anything that came into his head. It didn't matter what he said to her. Nearly all things were past Laurie's understanding. He had the impression that she had turned into parchment and was living on in that form. Her face was dry and webbed. She gazed at him from gentle old brown eyes. She was close to the end of a fortunate life.

His grandfather's well-being had depended for six decades on this serenely useless and submissive woman. I'm sorry, Laurie, he thought, you weren't useless. How could I say that, even to myself? Still, it was true that she had known fantastically little about the world. All she had understood was how to make a man happy, a small occupation—and how to make a martini. Maids stole from her; butchers, grocerymen, and all the tradespeople cheated her. She had chauffeurs and lap robes. She applauded at the curling matches when he, skip of the foursome, brought home a trophy to The Country Club. He wore heavy woolens and a tam-o'-shanter, as they all did for curling. The younger men displayed knickers and bulges of calf muscle. On weekdays they sold bonds and life insurance, and worked in the offices of grand steamship companies. The upper bourgeois merchants of Boston in that period married splendidly ignorant, pretty, dovelike ladies.

"Be careful, Laurie, it's a high curb."

"You're so strong." He was startled to hear her wispy voice. She was looking at him roguishly, and for a moment he was shocked.

"You know," his grandmother said in a whisper, "you're a very attractive young man."

"Laurie . . ."

She had gone back seventy years. He felt himself clad in brave whiskers, wearing a gold watch and chain looped from his vest. Eying him coquettishly, she declared in a singsong:

> "Man's life is a vapor
> And full of woes,
> He kicks a caper
> And down he goes."

"Laurie!" he said. "We're going home now."

His grandfather had been waiting on the porch.

"Gramps, I've got to leave this afternoon. I'm going back to New York!"

The old man looked puzzled. "Oh, when did you get here?"

THE FOOTBALL PLAYERS were gone from the Central Park playground, and the afternoon was becoming dark gray and cold. It would be December tomorrow. What had happened to Thanksgiving? He couldn't recall having tasted cranberry sauce. The holiday must somehow have passed him by—no, he had worked on a news roundup, that was it, and then gone drinking.

To kill off Sunday, he thought, I might as well go drinking again, but lightly. Get home early. Fly to Cape Cod in the morning without a hangover.

« 5 »

Memories of Genovese

AT THE ONE-O'CLOCK lunch hour Shannon's became noisier. The serious drinkers who had arrived at twelve were into their third rounds. The latecomers struggled for places at the bar and tried to catch up with them. From his table George had occasional glimpses of the new man at work when someone got off a stool or when the wall of heavy backs and bottoms parted for a moment. This man lacked the discreet nature of a good bartender. His scrabbly countenance was irritatingly there at all times, thrust amiably into conversations that were none of his business. Every so often when there was a lull he would open his mouth and let fall an offhand comment, and mop the bar, and grin and chuckle.

"How's that, sir?"

"Fine!"

"Want me to get a hot poker and mull it for you?"

Damn, George thought. He found himself becoming increasingly annoyed by the over-familiar servant. The man didn't belong at Shannon's.

IT HAD TAKEN George Pectin several years to change over into a Shannon's type of person. The conversion had been painless; he hadn't noticed it.

In the early 1950's during and after the Korean War his real self had been the scornful young man roaming Greenwich Village with the ones who had surpassed him now—such as Mack Hamlin, Hugh Brandt, Jan Crehore, and George Muchnik. In those years during each working day he took uptown the other, respectful self that made a living behind glass walls in Rockefeller Center. At night, switching selves at Fourteenth Street, he came back to the rebellion centering on the wild scenes in Bill Genovese's loft, and when the bop began and marijuana was passed around he was there.

Probably because of what happened to Genovese, he had without knowing it been frightened away from the Village scene. The rebel began to fade. Both selves remained, but the identity of the living Pectin moved uptown. It was true that the remnants of his assertive youth lingered on for a while, in a girl's apartment on Morton Street that he visited now and then. But he never slept overnight there, and one day she found somebody her own age and asked him not to come any more.

The night before his grandmother's funeral on Cape Cod he went down to the Village tentatively as a stranger for drinks and old times' sake. Out of habit he headed for the White Mule, the place of rebels where poets drank among the others, sometimes to death, and they were young there, it seemed, although they might be sixty. The young people clustered around the poets, old and young. It was a place of failure too, and of pathetic and fraudulent hangers-on, of mean little homosexuals as well as big expansive fags, of sour Irish intellectuals, discarded revolutionaries and scholars, pony-tailed girls, and thin dead-faced girls in black leotards who looked straight through someone from uptown; great muscular lads in sport shirts, brute poets; frail essayists and their wives, and (as if hired) a few beaming suburbanites to ignore.

George Pectin hesitated, looking in on this scene before entering. Once he had been part of it. Lounging against the bar, he had stared out at people like himself looking in, and their hopeful expressions had amused him. Now he pressed his nose against the dirty windowpane. He vaguely recognized one or two people, but saw no one who would be embarrassing.

He stood by the wall with a beer. Galantes and sportives a half-generation younger paraded before him. What a contrast between the White Mule and Shannon's. It's mostly in the stomachs, he thought, feeling his own. The washboard versus the pot. At Shannon's prosperity bellied up to the bar. The patrons there outweighed the skinny misfits at the White Mule fifteen or twenty pounds to a man. On the other hand, the habitués at Shannon's, with a few exceptions, couldn't go two rounds and probably not one with any man or girl at the White Mule. Not that the men at Shannon's had forgotten about girls, but their sexuality was diffused by liquor. The men at the White Mule got just as drunk, but were younger, in body and heart, thinner and hungrier, with hair-trigger sexual readiness, and in this bar when you moved the girls looked you in the eye.

George dodged her glance, because she was too young and following him in a businesslike way, and she was selling something, a pin. He shook his head quickly. A man near him accepted one, and so did another. He saw that the pin, which he had first imagined to be a campaign button of some kind, bore a message relating to world peace. She would be thrown out of Shannon's, he thought. Still he regretted that he hadn't taken one, even though he would never be able to wear it publicly.

He had several beers, sipping them alone and unobserved, feeling slightly more relaxed than at first. He thought to himself: It's ridiculous to apologize if it happens that one isn't rebellious any more. One can't go on indefinitely playing the role of self-conscious bohemian and rebel. One evolves. I belong in East Midtown, and am not

(43

ashamed, and will have a scotch, and not the bar scotch. I don't have to keep on drinking this lousy beer if I don't want to.

"A double scotch, please! Chivas Regal!"

An hour went by, and he became increasingly conscious of his soft stomach. He was tired and wished that somebody would give up a bar stool. Slender as he was, he didn't carry his weight well. His stomach pulled him forward. They said ten years before: "Turn Pectin sideways, and you can't see him." In those days he could run up five flights of stairs to Genovese's loft without panting.

The Negro man in a beret, puffing a pipe—he wouldn't get past the front door at Shannon's. Nor the blond young show-off who passed by with a clipboard of poems on his back. The board said: TAKE ONE. Nor the gypsy-dark girl with frightened eyes wearing a black sweater that fell almost to her knees. Nor the trio of supercilious young hoodlums with ringleted hair picking out the likeliest prospects to challenge in the alley behind the White Mule.

We were so much more interesting than these poseurs, thought George Pectin. For one thing, there had been a great deal of talent gathered in Bill Genovese's loft. One or two evenings a week he would go out, leaving Mary "for a little while," and join his friends there. None of the young writers and painters had yet produced anything, but they were about to. Secretly they were all at work.

Genovese's loft was sometimes strewn with broken glass. People made love in the bathroom (often, without realizing it, for a circle of spectators looking down from the skylight). They made love on the fire escape and on the roof. The music on the record player—either Italian opera, "The South Rampart Street Parade," or "The Navy" sung by the Andrews Sisters—was catastrophically loud to begin with, and was turned up gradually as the evening went on. The loft was divided into sections by translucent hanging screens, and there were unmade beds and cots everywhere. The light of a bare bulb shone in the kitchen by the fire escape, but as you moved into the loft's interior smaller amounts of light filtered through the screens, until at the far end it was a dark place. Here young philosophers sat on a window ledge. Clutching dirty coffee cups filled with Tallyho beer, or drinking blended whiskey from old jelly glasses, they looked out over the low roofs of Chelsea, and back into the room where shadowy people were cutting their feet on glass fragments, and Bill Genovese ate glass, and music roared out of the dark.

One night in the kitchen George felt a hand on his elbow. Bill Genovese beckoned mysteriously to him. "Come up on the roof. I want to show you my garden!" His brown eyes were alight with crazy good humor and he grinned at George's hesitation. They climbed by way of the fire escape. "The South Rampart Street Parade" thundered below them. Bill Genovese's curly hair fell over his forehead as he paused at the skylight to inspect something going on in the bathroom. He motioned for George to look, but George would not. It was dark on the roof and a soft rain was falling. They ducked among taut wires and passed under an old water tank. A frightening thing about this roof was that it simply went off into dark space. Along the edge of the gutter, from boxes filled with earth, flowered tulips and pansies.

"Do you like them, George Pectin? Come closer and look."

"I can see them from here," George said. "I like them from here."

Bill Genovese walked carelessly along the edge of the roof, saying: "It would be easy to fall off, wouldn't it?"

"Yes, better be careful," George heard himself reply in a voice that he carefully held steady.

The handsome face suddenly drew near. Genovese squatted on his heels and whispered: "I've asked you up here for a reason. Only you. Why don't you push me off?"

"I couldn't do that, Bill."

"Why not? You don't like me. But nobody else knows that. It's slippery here. With you, they'd believe it was an accident. Push me off, George!"

"I like you well enough, Bill."

Other voices came out on the roof. Bill Genovese laughed and once again walked to the edge. A boy and girl, both of whom loved him, rushed forward together and pulled him back down on the tar paper and kissed him, and George silently withdrew and made his way down the fire escape.

And they were off again, at any time of day or night. The solemn teletype operator who didn't speak, but who

followed Bill Genovese everywhere a few paces behind,
always had his car. There would be shouts. "Come on!"
"Let's go, Jay boy!" The car would roll. Bill Genovese
might, for instance, start to get out of the car while it was
speeding along. The teletype man would put on the brakes.
Bill Genovese would strip aerials from a line of cars. With
a fistful of aerials he would approach a car pulled up at a
stop light, hold them out to the mute and staring occu-
pants, inquiring: "Would you like to buy a radio?"

Then, on Sixth Avenue, might come the satirical ballet
performed in front of a phalanx of onrushing taxis bearing
down on him six-deep, before which, in a terrifying parody
of non-violence, he would lie down—and somehow amid
shouts, horns, and screaming brakes they would miss him,
and he would get up and dust himself off, grinning, his
wild, merry eyes dancing, as his friends rushed to embrace
him.

Genovese, on the waterfront, entering a barroom full of
longshoremen, stepped up to the nearest one, saying: "Give
me a big, wet kiss!" kissed him, and walked slowly out
unharmed; out of money, laboring all night in a dough
factory, staggering home at dawn, leaping on the running
board of a bakery truck to shout at the driver: "I hate
bread!"

He was puerile, foolish and gaily cruel: on a rough
flight to Provincetown, the most courteous passenger, suddenly an imitation steward, coming down the aisle with a
huge paper bag, bowing to a gray-faced man: "Sir, would
you prefer to be sick now or later?"; to a team of neatly

uniformed oil company trainees running to their pumps: "Up your ass with Mobilgas!"; in Schrafft's cocktail lounge, as the old ladies dallied with their big martinis: "I want to fuck George Pectin!" or, to present an adoring girl: "George Pectin, meet Henrietta, the worst lay in New York. She knows nothing about feminine hygiene."

But his gaiety gave way at times to fearful depressions. Nothing could be more depressing than a black afternoon in Bill Genovese's loft when visitors dropping by in search of excitement found him small and unshaven, huddled amid the ruins of a party held days before, surrounded by slop, dead cigarettes, and unmade beds, staring at the wall. He might remain in this condition for days. Slowly his spirits would regenerate. Nothing would happen, and still nothing, and then perhaps out of another dead day he would snatch a random, despairing joke, seize on some improvised intent, and leap back into life. First would come the pantomime and acrobatics. Followed by a gaggle of laughing, terrified friends, he emerged hand-over-hand out of the deep subway, climbing along the partition between the up and down escalators. Next was seen a line of citizens on the down escalator, vacant-faced or absorbed in their newspapers, and all at once among the faces a pair of feet upthrust, with those descending before unaware of the handstand behind their backs and those coming after, embarrassed, dismayed, half-grins on their faces, turning to one another for reassurance.

Now Genovese decided to walk through New York City in an absolutely straight line, no matter what. Up he went, shinnying up a Third Avenue El pillar, over the tracks, down the other side, across the street, up and over the hood of a parked truck, clambering like a trampolinist over the canvas cover, down again . . . and suddenly his intent was coupled with a second obsession. This was to get to a party to which they all were carefully and specifically uninvited. Miraculously the straight line led to the door of the forbidden apartment; the bell was rung furiously, the door opened a crack, and Genovese with his followers pressing behind him fell forward across the threshold as if establishing a beachhead, and the avalanche of his friends toppled in behind him so that a wave of rejected humanity appeared to have broken and crashed into the foyer.

Bill Genovese had been right. George Pectin didn't really like him. He was too afraid of him. In the beginning, on his first visit to the loft, George was shocked by the clamor and abandon around him, and walked about with an attitude of frozen disapproval. Genovese shouted: "You're different. You don't like us. You've got a death's head!" and scaled a twelve-inch 78 record across the room, barely missing George's temple. But later he grinned and chattered as if nothing had happened, and George became an accepted hanger-on. He didn't want to hang around. He was a little ashamed of the fascination that drew him to the loft, but he came back again and again.

Now, a stranger in the White Mule, George Pectin remembered the parties: drumming on kitchen pots all night long, and drinking from jugs of red wine; floating with hinges in his joints, his feet hardly seeming to touch the floor of the loft; listening to Wild Bill Davis on the organ when a girl drummer reached out with her stick and, not missing a beat, smashed his glass of wine, and he had to drink out of spikes. Through all this survived the grinning presence of Genovese: kicking a crippled boy to make him feel acceptable, lying down drunk in haystacks, climbing up fire escapes, peeping in the open windows, relating gleefully how a man making love turned from his girl to inquire casually: "What's your trouble, Bud?"

He remembered too a steaming night on the rooftop above George Muchnik's place in East Harlem. Dawn came with a sprinkle of rain. He was kissing a little girl who wanted to go into the travel business, and Muchnik was playing a beautiful, snarling side called "Hispano Harlem" by Morton Gould. At daybreak the city was smoking in the rain. They could see a haze on the rivers and, all at once against the black chimneys, Bill Genovese with his arms outspread dancing on the edge of the roof.

At that time an old longing had come back to George Pectin: the voluptuous nightmare of the woman, dark, strong, and menacing as Calypso, who was going to envelop him. Unexpectedly she came out of the summer night. As he had in his crib, he woke up frightened, shrinking from her presence. Yet there was nothing he wanted more than to be caught and held in the cave. Even when he lay fully awake in the dark, there remained the indistinct menace and joy of this woman with bright eyes and great heavy limbs watching him expectantly.

One night, walking on cobblestones, he passed a bar full of despairing people with their heads in their arms. A bleak light took away their shadows. The bartender was staring blankly at the far wall, with rows of unwashed beer glasses before him. And George saw her. A huge powerful Negro woman stood triumphantly among the sufferers, and she called out to someone: "I hold court here!" He paused, and his heart turned over, because her bright eyes had met his, and she was smiling. Then a voice called out: "Vivian!" She looked away to answer, and George Pectin, outside, hurriedly walked on. But he was trembling, almost unconscious with desire by the time he arrived home.

He tossed in bed, and had a huge, unbearable sex dream, and woke exhausted. The day passed in a fever. His hands were all but palsied on the typewriter, and he could hardly wait for the dark.

But he couldn't remember where the place was. There had been no sign in front, and he had no clue but that of the great dark woman holding court. He ran through the crooked streets, and up an alley. In a doorway Bill Genovese was watching him with a mischievous smile. George stood before him, wavering in his frayed shirt, uncreased pants, and sneakers, and implored, as if expecting Genovese to understand his dream: "Vivian!"

Genovese showed no surprise. Nodding, he beckoned George to follow. Both wearing sneakers, they ran out of the silent alley. George stumbled and panted to keep up. They ran down many streets. All at once his guide stopped and pointed, and after a moment silently raced off. He was in front of the ruined bar, as before, and Vivian stood in the doorway waiting for him.

But she couldn't see him. No, not this weekend. She spoke in a soft, fluting accent. Darling, I have a date. But next week! Oh, yes. You're cute. Why are you shaking? Let me hold your hand. Why, he's so cold. What are you afraid of, darling? Next week. You come down. Her suddenly fierce eyes roved over him, and he became aware of what she must think of a thin, trembling white boy with circles under his eyes. She caught his wrist, and drew him to her.

"How can I find you?"

She smiled. You won't have any trouble finding me. *I hold court here.*

Over the weekend a dreadful event took place.

TRAILING A CROWD of disciples, who followed him in dismay and fascination, Bill Genovese mischievously courted death. Everyone saw that he was dancing before death like a lover, to seduce death if he could, and kid her, cavort in her arms and get away intact, grinning, just out of reach. It seemed that death was bemused by her impudent suitor, in no hurry to possess him, and like a great cat pleased to let him escape and run around.

When he died it might have been imagined that death herself was shocked, taken unawares by his sudden end. It was foolish and horrible. He was in the subway late at night with people he didn't know very well. Then he didn't want to go to the Bronx after all. He tried to climb out of the subway car as the train started rolling out of the station. The train moved too quickly for him. His belt buckle caught on the window frame and he couldn't pull back into the car in time to get away from the oncoming pillar.

The next day when the paragraph came out in the *Daily News* that a man identified as William Genovese, 27, had halted subway service for an hour on the Lexington Avenue line when he accidentally fell to his death in the Bleecker Street station, Vivian ran sobbing in the streets of the Village until she fell in exhaustion. She spent several days in the hospital, and when she came out kept to herself, and was not seen in her bar or any such place for many weeks.

Everyone had known that Bill Genovese was dear to her, but not that she had loved him that much. Meanwhile George Pectin moved uptown.

« *6* »

An Encounter with "Bad News" Muchnik

THOSE DAYS IN Greenwich Village and Chelsea had been deceptive for George Pectin. The ones he caroused with in Genovese's loft and at the White Mule were working behind his back. While he completed his proper editorial day at *Forecast*, they worked on books, plays, and poems, and on paintings. He put in time on his book too, but not much. There was no hurry. It didn't occur to him that he and his friends would ever have to grow older. Then, one by one, they broke the rules. George Muchnik, whose trial flights of hatred and obscenity had seemed to George Pectin little more than disgusting, one year simply scared away on gigantic wings and became a great young poet, and he was talked about all over the world. Hugh Brandt sold out a one-man show on Fifty-seventh Street. Jan Crehore inspired America's young people with a big, traveling novel that he wrote in two months.

The night Mack Hamlin came to his apartment with considerately muted joy to announce that he had won a national prize contest for first novels, George (after Mack had gone) buried his head in his arms and cried.

"If they're right, I'm wrong!" he shouted to Mary Pectin. "The whole pack of them; they've bummed and scrounged and lived off women, and never done a day's work beyond the menial. Never had the guts to look for a real job. Never lived up to their responsibilities. Look at me! Saddled! With you!"

He had run out of the apartment and downstairs on a cold December day, popping in and out of bars as though attached to a paddle. He wound up at the White Mule and fell asleep there.

Now, so MANY YEARS LATER, George was conscious of a stir in the White Mule. Several noisy people had just entered. There was a jostling and the sound of a big, confident voice with a rabble of lesser voices escorting it. A girl with blue-black hair rolling about her shoulders, who reminded him of a younger Gretchen, came out of the throng and made for George. She wore a black sweater and skirt. Her dark brows crossed with a vertical line above her nose when she scowled, and her close-set eyes were fixed on him. She carried a board with flapping papers affixed to it, and George saw that these pages were filled with signatures.

"Sir," the dark girl accosted him in a soft voice, "will you sign the protest against bombing helpless Asians?"

"I'm sorry. I can't just sign a petition without reading it. Besides, I don't like—"

"Oh, read it, please, sir! At the top. Here!"

He was aware of others crowding around, silently pressuring him. He tried to explain with a smile: "I'm in no position—"

"You have no position?" She studied him expressionlessly, and said: "I understand you, sir."

"But you probably don't!" he cried. "And I wish, please . . ."

"Hi there, sir! World Peace too wild for you?"

After ten years he would naturally have to encounter George Muchnik at such a moment. But then Muchnik was always present during the crisis and embarrassments of others—or if he was not, had "just been with" the sufferer, or he arrived a few minutes after the event. In this instance George suspected that Muchnik had sicked the girl on him.

"Hello, Muchnik. I'm not a petition-signer, that's all."

" 'Muchnik!' " cried the poet, in pain. "How weird my last name sounds when spoken with such frosty disap-

proval. Old friend and comrade!" He offered a handshake
that couldn't be refused, and his gleaming, sardonic eyes
considered George Pectin. "Why so formal?"

George saw that Muchnik now had a tattered army of
admirers following him about. The group he had brought
into the White Mule was made up of a half-dozen slovenly,
bright-eyed boys and girls, and a ferociously attentive lady
of about fifty years with straight platinum-blond hair and
bangs. Muchnik and his friends had obviously taken part in
a peace demonstration. The poet was exhilarated, as though
he had been arrested, recognized, and released.

"Why so formal? First with her," said Muchnik, indicating the girl who was collecting signatures at the other
end of the bar. "Now with me. Is it the formality of fear?
Of illness?" He peered sympathetically at George Pectin.
"You have a reluctant hand. You look pale. Are you all
right?"

"I'm feeling very well," responded George angrily. "Or
rather I was before you came."

"Rejection! After ten years, I meet fear and loathing in
your glance. But you mustn't fear us." The poet swept out
his arm to embrace the boys and girls around him. "You
only have to be afraid of Mae. She's the reincarnation of
Socrates."

"A pleasure." George bowed with nervous irony to the
woman with bangs.

"And do you not, Protagoras, pursue after pleasure as
a good, and avoid pain as an evil?" she replied, glaring at
him.

(57

"I beg your pardon?"

"However, Protagoras, if you call pleasure an evil in relation to some other standard, you will be able to show us that standard. But you have none to show."

George Pectin looked pleadingly at Muchnik, who said in a genial tone: "Don't worry. You'll be all right if she doesn't get you in a corner. But I'm concerned about you. What have you been doing with yourself?"

"I'm still with the magazine."

" 'The magazine!' How sorrowfully you put it. Observe!" George Muchnik said to his friends. "The subtle savageries of Babylon are visited upon us in marvelous ways. The doctors of compromise can eviscerate a man and sew him up again. You see him walking around in his Brooks Brothers suit, and never guess that—"

"This isn't a Brooks Brothers suit, Muchnik. I'm surprised that you would use such a cliché. Also I'm not eviscerated, spiritually or otherwise. It isn't necessary to walk around in dirty clothes and smoke marijuana in order to be genuine. Of course, I'm sure you think that being famous or notorious gives you a license—"

"Fame is money! Release! JOY!" shouted the poet, waving his arms.

"Dear Alcibiades," the lady with bangs pushed in, giving him an adoring look. "Have Protagoras, the sophist, inform us against what dangers the courageous are ready to go— against the same dangers as cowards?"

"Be kind, sweet Mae. Don't let a man's expensive suit obscure his agony. Forgive us!" The poet ducked his head in the charming imitation of humility that George Pectin remembered very well. "It's not fair to put you down when you've suffered more than anyone. Wait! There's a table. I'll get some beers and we'll talk."

AFTER NEARLY TEN YEARS the two qualities that he feared in George Muchnik remained unchanged. The first was a general atmosphere of tension and bad news that he carried with him, and the second was his scandalous over-familiarity.

As a young graduate student, Bad News Muchnik was the bearer of nervous tidings. His messages tended to inspire doubt and fear. When Bill Genovese was killed in the subway it was Muchnik who first heard about his death. When somebody was hit by a truck, wept over his lost girl, or tried to kill himself, the young poet was likely to be nearby.

Once George Pectin was in the hospital after a tonsillectomy. The wound had hemorrhaged. He was under drugs and fever, and his throat was a globe of pain. It was late at night and all the nurses seemed to have left the hospital, and he felt that he was going to die. A dark presence stood in the doorway looking at him. George tried to drive Muchnik away but couldn't utter a sound. He pressed the nurse's buzzer but no one came. Muchnik was standing in the doorway, talking to him in an offhand manner. George, writhing from the pain in his throat, had no idea what he said. Finally Muchnik waved goodbye and left. The nurse came in angrily demanding what was the matter. He couldn't speak—nor would he have been able to explain his feeling of apprehension. A friend had come in to say hello. . . .

Muchnik used uneasiness as his ally. Frequently he would contribute a destructive whisper. Thus, when George Pectin was doing his best to make an impression on a girl, he received the news softly in one ear: "You've got bad breath!" Or on another occasion: "Why the bags under your eyes?" Then, following this sabotage, came the head-bobbing humility and boyish disavowal of aggression.

George remembered during the McCarthy years a wire service photograph of Dean Acheson, taken just after his tormentor, the senator from Wisconsin, had gotten into an elevator with him. The photographer had caught on the Senator's face a joyous sneering laugh. In contrast, the beleaguered Secretary of State was staring high and straight before him with a taut upper lip that drew his mustache into a thread.

Muchnik always made George feel like Dean Acheson in the elevator. Muchnik's presence in a room signaled the impossibility of anyone on the scene maintaining a dignified reserve. There would always be his over-familiar laugh; the bold eyes probing for a show of doubt. He didn't hesitate to ask the most personal question. He was a provocateur of confidences, and made use of the information he obtained to guide nervous people to the edge of their self-esteem and on occasion push them off.

Muchnik camped in humility, George Pectin believed.

By stripping others of their protective dignity, he became superior to them, for he himself was accustomed to feeling strange and an outsider. Others such as George Pectin had no reason to engage in a swap of confidences, the romp in the mud of truth, because they had so much more to lose than he.

Hence, in George Pectin's opinion, Muchnik's game was to prey on others' self-respect. He seemed bound and determined to make everybody around him break down and confess, break into senseless laughter or cry, give up all pretense, expose themselves utterly. If he could, Muchnik created an anarchy of shameless scenes, in which everything normally private became public. You got down and made love in the open, and so forth.

The last time George Pectin had seen him, at a friend's house for dinner, his friend's wife had laid out a formal meal with the best silver and a tablecloth. Seated next to the boy he had brought along, Muchnik had placed his hand flat on the clean plate before him, and grinned. The boy had ceremoniously put salt and pepper on the hand and started to carve it up. Muchnik, grinning, withdrew his hand from the plate, which was about to be passed to the hostess, filled up with food, and presumably given to someone with Muchnik's hand imprint, a drop of blood, and salt and pepper still on it. George swore to himself: if that plate comes to me, I'm going to refuse it. As things worked out, the hostess switched the china around so that Muchnik ended up with his own print and spot of blood beneath the ham and raisin sauce, but the *petit guignol* was (it seemed)

(*61*

so purposelessly upsetting that George lost his appetite.

Despite this sort of behavior, one unrelenting truth had to be acknowledged. The one who disturbed him so possessed a blazing, and from George's standpoint, unforgivable poetic talent uncomfortably close to genius. If he was drawn to the humiliation of others, and sometimes assisted in it, he also had an immense feeling for them once it became evident that they had suffered. Then he was extraordinarily tender. When someone had no hope left, and broke down, he was gentle. He cared enormously what happened to the meanest individuals—in this way he gave the sufferers dignity of a sort, by noticing them so carefully.

He began with the muse of hatred. Now, George Pectin observed ten years later in the White Mule, one remarkable change had taken place in Muchnik. Having reviled his times and been honored for it, the poet had raged out of his dark strangeness and become attractive. As though hatred in the process of becoming art had cleaned his pores and increased his circulation, he now had a positive radiance. There was a new, if still dangerous, gentleness about him. He had become a charming trouble-maker.

THE THIRTY-FIVE-YEAR-OLD REBEL approached him carrying beers. Muchnik's youthful followers sat around the table gravely studying George Pectin. One, with a tower of curly blond hair, broke into a giggle and hid his face in George Muchnik's lap. Muchnik cupped his hands

about the boy's face and kissed him. The woman Mae
continued to stare at George Pectin. He felt out of place
and uncomfortable, seeing that many of the drinkers at
the bar were watching their table, knowing him to be from
uptown.

"You know one of the reasons why you're annoyed at
me?"

"I'm not especially annoyed at you, Muchnik."

"We have the same first name. When we're in the same
room and somebody calls out 'George!' you feel nervous
and violated if they're talking to me. And they usually are.
I've seen the look of annoyance cross your face. I can
hear you thinking: 'What is this obnoxious fellow whose
father came from Vitebsk doing with my good Christian
name? George, slayer of dragons! . . .' "

"None of that is true, as you well know, Muchnik."

But it was slightly true. He was thinking that his grandfather had never gone through any trouble with Muchniks,
and had no idea that they existed. He would have dismissed
him as a Bolshevik!

"You, George Pectin, descendant of Norman and Scottish chieftains! I remember with tenderness a drunken talk
we had in which you expressed your terror of being violated. I could see then nearly ten years ago that you would
do almost anything—or refrain from doing almost anything—to escape having your dignity reduced. But the
irony is, you who feared violation more than any of us
have been violated most grievously."

"According to you, Muchnik, anyone who has held

down a job and supported his family, in spite of not wanting to, has in some mysterious way 'sold out.' But do you
know what? I'm aware that it will sound ridiculous, but in
spite of your talent and accomplishments, which I do not
deny, I think that in some respects you're envious."

The poet leaned forward sympathetically, it appeared,
and whispered: "You never did finish your book!"

"I still have time."

"You're too tense, working on that foolish magazine."

"Maybe I am."

"Maybe . . ." The dark ironical presence before him
became kindly and serious. ". . . It would release your
creative juices if somebody took you home and went down
on you. Take Artie here."

The blond boy who had put his face in George Muchnik's lap lifted up his head. George Pectin put down his
drink and shoved his chair back.

"You look horrified," the poet said. "Come on, it's not
so serious. If you don't want him, take Serena."

A girl with a cute, lascivious expression regarded him
merrily.

There was nothing to do but leave.

"Muchnik," he said, "you've got me in a bad position,
and characteristically you exploit it. All right, there's
nothing I can say at the moment. I give you credit. Your
so-called 'holy revolution'—somehow you people brought
it off. But tell me!" he called after the poet who had
leaped up to throw his arms around someone. "What's so
holy about you?"

"*They dared! . . .*"

"An uprising of misfits, sadists, psychopaths! It won't last long! If there's any justice—"

"*But you didn't!*"

He turned to discover standing behind his chair a prim little creature about twenty years old, a cross-eyed girl wearing thick-lensed glasses.

"I've had to be decent and responsible," he said.

"Because it was more important to you."

"Decency *is* important."

She piped again, like her little sister reciting at school: "They dared! You didn't!"

"Bitch!" He pushed her, and she fell to the floor. "Oh, my God, I'm terribly sorry!" He leaped up and his chair went over backwards. "I'm sorry, I shouldn't have done that!" He helped her up, explaining: "You see, you hurt my feelings. Why did you have to say what you did?"

She looked at him, cross-eyed and expressionless, and answered: "Because it's true!"

Muchnik was in the middle of a crowd of admirers and lovers. "Call me!" he shouted over their heads. "I'm in the book!"

As George started to hurry out of the White Mule, the woman Mae stepped in front of him.

"Well, then, Protagoras, you cite holiness and justice. Do you consider that they have a degree of likeness?"

"Please, I have to . . ."

She placed her finger on his chest, and glaring from under the platinum bangs, demanded: "Have you ever admitted that holiness is *not* of the nature of justice, nor justice of the nature of holiness, and that the poet is holy and independent of justice, and you are just and independent of holiness, and that, Protagoras, you can't be both?"

He said: "If that is true, then all I've been taught is wrong," and she answered: "Oh, Sophist, all you *have* been taught is wrong."

At this he walked past her and went out, hailing a taxicab in the dark street.

« 7 »

He Kicks a Caper

SHANNON'S HAD BEGUN folding up for the afternoon. It was nearly two-thirty. The few drinkers remaining at the bar had no choice but to hear Philip Rhodes, the editorial voice, declaim: ". . . Christian revival! . . ." The shaggy-haired bartender laid a finger against his nose and openly smiled at this proposition. Vito the manager gave the new man a somber look.

"Joey, I've had it," George Pectin murmured to the old waiter. "Could you bring me a cup of coffee, please."

He had been making an odd bargain with time. He

would settle for being already dead if he could have been young and happy in the time of his grandparents' youth. He would settle for already lying peacefully in a country graveyard if, at the time of his death, he had been able to believe that at the end of his long sleep there would come the day of resurrection. He would gladly accept dying if at the last instant he could embrace eternal life. As it was, the alcoholic immortality of his lunch hour was what kept him going, at the same time slowly destroyed him, which was the same thing.

To REACH THE CAPE COD TOWN where he had spent his summers as a boy George had to change buses several times. Each bus was smaller than the preceding one. The towns he passed through seemed to become progressively miniaturized, until at last when he alighted from the little bus that served the town of his memory he stepped into a toy village, and walking down Main Street toward his grandfather's house he felt as a child.

The event—his grandmother's being put underground in a box—was much too big for him. Although he worked for a magazine devoted to current and future events, he was out of touch with death and didn't know a great deal about it. On Manhattan Island, his sanctuary, people more or less vanished and were likely to be buried somewhere else. On that island you seldom heard a church bell tolling for any reason. Going back to one's home town, back to one's boyhood, and finding death there, was quite a different matter. He was innocent of death, and increasingly afraid of the moment when he would embrace his grandfather. At some point, the only authoritative person in his life would cry. He thought resentfully: There ought to be a better way to handle this kind of thing.

Yet as he walked through the town the presence of death gave him a curiously sweet feeling of homesickness that he hadn't experienced on other visits. All at once he felt easier, and his childhood came back in the form of delightful, familiar things: crushed clam shells in the gutter, dried periwinkles, and the smell of clams and fish, a single outboard motor buzzing in the harbor attached to a tilted-up dory moving out under the gray, ribbed overcast; the fisherman in a black slicker reaching for the bait box.

An old cutting, sighing sound vibrated from Ladd's sawmill. Walking under the elms, George ran his hand along the top of the white picket fence bordering the lawn in front of his grandfather's house. When he was six years old he had first gazed between these same pickets, imagining that the wheels of passing automobiles were spinning backwards.

His aging relatives and friends from the town were gathered on the lawn. Their breaths mingled in the cool afternoon. He waved at a few of them and walked up the steps to the front porch. He walked up past the wooden crow that had been perched on the railing since he could remember, and saw his grandfather. The old man was standing alone in the open air. Everyone remained at a distance from him, and he was not looking at anybody.

The old man wasn't crying. He leaned on his cane and stared out over the lawn. More than anything, he seemed puzzled by what was going on. He seemed ready to call out: "Now, see here, just a moment . . ." and wave his cane at the morticians, demanding: "What are those fellows doing here? I don't know them!"

He clasped George warmly but didn't speak. George observed that his grandfather was impatient, and wished that they would all go home so that he and his wife could be together.

A little woman cousin touched his elbow. "How is your wife, George? That lovely girl! What a terrible thing! I'm so glad to hear she's better. And your little boy is staying with Janet. How nice of her!"

He was sorry to learn that his sister hadn't been able to come. He could have talked to her about Davey; they could have reminded each other of family history. They might have stolen a few shots of vodka together. As it was, he sneaked a few swallows in the bathroom and, being alone, felt somewhat guilty about it.

"Oh, yes. George is doing very well. He works on *Forecast* magazine."

"Poor dear. She knew nothing. It was a blessing."

He prowled upstairs and encountered the Italian housekeeper whom he had heard whispers about. In the past year she was said to have had an increasing influence on his grandfather. In the absence of other members of the family, she had (it was said) worked stealthily to turn the old man against his sons and daughters. She was plump and gray-haired and in tears. She had been refused permission to sit in the family pew. She wept on George's arm and said that she read his magazine every week.

In the little salt-box Episcopal church the organ groaned, a bell pealed, members of the bereaved family bowed their heads and wept, the morticians stood about gazing at the floor and the earth; the coffin with its poor dumb cargo waited nearby, and the handsome young minister declared:

"I know that my redeemer liveth . . ."

He added in a resonant, even trembling, baritone that

"though this body be destroyed, yet shall I see God: whom I shall see for myself, and mine eyes shall behold, and not as a stranger . . ."

George Pectin was seated in the third row. Looking at the back of his grandfather's head and the other bowed-down heads, he cried along with the others, and wished that he were back in New York. The helplessness of humanity was too much. Sooner or later all of these people would be packed into similar boxes. Why try to dignify the farce? He remembered the beginning of the "message" his grandfather had labored over at midnight:

I believe there is a Creator of this World. There must be a Creator when you see the wonderful anatomy of All Human Beings & all Animals . . .

(71

But a few paragraphs later on the honest old man had confessed:

I don't know everything about Life. I don't know why we are here in this World but do know we live and die.

He remembered his grandmother's final coquettry:

Man's life is a vapor
And full of woes . . .

The young minister interrupted:

"My soul fleeth unto the Lord before the morning watch! . . ."

From her box his grandmother's whispery little voice seemed to answer:

He kicks a caper
And down he goes

And he also imagined a harsh chuckle, and then another voice coming from the depths of the church behind the altar, saying derisively: "A long line of Norman and Scottish chieftains!" He visualized intruding on his grandfather's suffering the grinning, revolutionary image of Muchnik, simply there, watching, as he had that agonizing night in the hospital.

The minister, young Reverend Payne, shook the tears from his eyes. He turned the pages of his prayer book in an almost panicky way as though his mind had gone blank.

Then he looked out at the mourners and said: "A sweet and blameless life has been taken from us!"

George Pectin's grandfather stood up supported by his two sons, and slowly made his way to the aisle, and they guided him very slowly along the carpet toward the outdoors where the morticians and the limousines were waiting. The old man's staring old eyes saw nothing, but his dignity was intact. He still wasn't crying. As he passed by, no more than a foot away, young George let go completely. Sobs that he didn't know he was capable of came out in great heaves.

The limousines wound through the cemetery. George hung his head out of the window until he felt better. Odd memories of the old man in the front car bobbed up in his mind. One amazing thing was that his grandfather as a little boy had actually seen Charles Dickens. He also remembered the first telephone that rang in Scotland and the first incandescent bulb to be displayed in Glasgow.

One evening a few summers before, George had come into the Cape Cod living room. His grandfather who had laid eyes on Dickens was watching not only television but Bobby Darin. There was a perplexed look on the old man's veined countenance. The song was "Mack the Knife." Darin skipped an invisible jump rope, contemptuously snapped his fingers and laughed. The old man started to ask George something, but then shook his head and went on looking at the screen.

A cold wind blew at the grave site. It fluttered the veils of the women and stirred the folds of their black dresses.

The old man's cane was apparently useless and he was being held upright by his sons. His scant, feathery hair seemed on the verge of blowing away. A rug of artificial grass lay by the grave. The pall-bearers were about to lower the shining box into the earth, and his grandfather uttered some kind of outcry that the wind took from George's hearing.

The minister caressed his forehead as if he had been taken with a fever, but struggled on with the ritual:

"cometh up, and is cut down, like a flower."

Someone's elbow accidentally touched a limousine horn.

"Of whom," asked the Reverend Payne angrily.

"may we seek for succor, but of thee, O Lord, who for our sins are justly displeased?"

*Man's life is a vapor
And full of woes.*

"Yet, O Lord God most holy, O Lord most mighty, O holy and merciful savior, deliver us not into the pains of eternal death. . . ."

He kicks a caper . . .

AT SHANNON's the cup of coffee helped. Philip Rhodes, the editorial writer, had put on his raincoat and clapped somebody on the back.

"So long, Vito!"

"Goodbye, gemmun, thank you."

George Pectin saw that he was the only remaining customer. Vito and Joey the waiter had their backs politely turned. Only the new barman, polishing glasses, took direct notice of him with a humorously disapproving shake of his head.

"Joey!"

Outside the afternoon had suddenly become light. The rain had stopped, and clearing skies told him to get going. He sweated in the cool gusts coming out of the west. Splinters of sunlight flashed in his path, and there were little furrowed waves in all the puddles.

He had time yet. A little courage, and he would be free. Horns brayed up and down the avenue. The city thundered and splashed after the rain, and the sign before him glittered: WALK.

PART II « *Trains* »

« 8 »

By This Time You Must Have Realized

THE TRAIN IN WHICH George Pectin was riding moved toward the end of a warm, sunny Christmas afternoon. It rolled along the Connecticut shoreline past wet fields and limp brush on the way to Bridgeport and New York. Sun all day long had dissolved the snow crust into brimming ponds.

Christmas had been exhausted hours ago. Many of the passengers sprawled out with their eyes closed; others did their best to remain upright, their faces sweating with fatigue. Piled above their heads, bulging out of the luggage racks, was a car-length jumble of presents. Wrappings hung down from the racks and danced in tatters to the motion of the train.

George Pectin rode in the smoking compartment, which was partially separated from the rest of the car by glass-walled extensions. He was one of an odd lot. Near the door sat two Chinese men. One was old and shrunken behind his glasses; the other, perhaps his son, wore a merchant sea-man's black sweater and rolled his own cigarettes. Across the aisle two Hungarians, after greeting one another— "*Servus!*"—talked incomprehensibly and then fell silent. Next to them a vacuous sailor boy gently chewed his gum.

George fretted for lack of a newspaper. There was no club car on the train. He could only look for minutes on end at the same people. The Hungarians smiled at nothing. The sailor examined his cigarette lighter for the hundredth time.

George's mouth was bitter from smoking, but he couldn't stop, and inserted one more cigarette between his lips. Once again Mary's image appeared before him: how she had bloomed and laughed by the sanatorium Christmas tree.

At Christmas time his wife had always made him feel like Scrooge. The humbug of a single day's decency, pear tree and plump partridges, peace on earth (all right!), the in-conceivable birth, his own resurrection that would not come off, the compulsive swaps of merchandise, torn

wrappings, and ah's of delight, invariably made him want
to stand on one leg and then the other.

But he was a stranger at all ceremonies. They were imi-
tations of, and poor excuses for, immortality. The idea
was that men pass, ceremonies remain. George Pectin
didn't intend to be distracted by such nonsense. No
parade-ground ritual, explosion of firecrackers, dance
around the maypole, or crashing of beer mugs together
and singing a faternal song would be permitted to confuse
the issue. That went for Christmas as well. It went for his
wife as well. He would be free of them, and no amount of
holiday decency, soul, tradition, or peace on earth would
deter him.

BRIDGEPORT CAME ON in the twilight. Passengers got off and
others climbed aboard. One man stumbled into the smoking
compartment with two heavy suitcases and a golf bag. He
seemed at the end of his strength. After a tottering effort
he managed to stow his belongings in the luggage cabinet at
the end of the car. The train started with a jolt and he
nearly fell over.

He plunged into the men's room, and emerged a minute
later with his face wet and mottled, smiling apologetically.
The Hungarians, the Chinese, and the sailor eyed him. He
must be, George Pectin guessed, between forty and fifty, a
professor of some kind, a man of gentle background.
Dressed in a sports jacket and, curiously enough, formal

black trousers, he was an immediately ludicrous man, gangling, with innocent light-blue eyes, and hair the color of damp straw hanging down over his forehead. He looked about him winking. It was a tic of anguish, yet his despair had a ridiculous quality.

One of his thin hands gripped the corners of the partition. The other fumbled at a crushed pack of Kents. The first cigarette his fingers discovered was broken in half. Unknowingly he tried to light it. Twice, three times, he applied the lighter flame before realizing his mistake.

With an apologetic smile all around, he stumbled to a chair. Even here his affliction, whatever it might be, wouldn't let him rest. His cheek twitched. He pulled his tie loose. He twisted his neck to look out of the window. He looked out at the night where nothing could be seen but bright dots beyond the woods and black shapes passing. He watched these for a long time. Ashes fell on his rumpled trousers. His Adam's apple bobbed, and he gave a small cough. Smoking seemed gradually to calm him, but once just before the train pulled into Stamford, he slapped the heel of his palm against his forehead and cried out.

The brief stop brought a new smoker into the compartment. She came weaving down the aisle, trailing a black leather handbag behind her, letting it scrape along the floor. She sat across from the Hungarians and the sailor, and glared at them. Covertly George saw her attention rest on the anguished professor, who had just dropped his cigarette on the floor, picked it up, and was now staring at it fearfully.

"Ah, go ahead and smoke it! What do you care?" the woman said.

Hastily with his self-deprecating smile, he nodded to her and quickly smoked. But his hands were trembling and he wouldn't look at anyone.

The woman of fifty winters, red-faced, surly and bold, took her time settling down. First she propped her handbag on the empty chair beside her. Then she found a small silver-plated flask and drank from it. As much a bag as what she carried along with her, trailing her dissipations behind her as she pleased, she scrutinized George, the Chinese, Hungarians, and the sailor boldly, and didn't care, but when her gaze returned to the unhappy man across from her she looked at him differently.

"Christmas!" she declared loudly to all of the men in the compartment. George Pectin made himself so dull as to be invisible. The Hungarians looked at her blankly; the Chinese smiled; the sailor yawned. The ridiculous professor glanced up at her in alarm.

"It's Christmas, and people should talk to each other!" the woman said. "I'm not going all the way into New York just looking at you fellows. I want to talk to somebody." Her finger shot out and she pointed to the man George Pectin thought of as the professor, and she announced: "I choose . . . you!"

He stammered, and finally said: "Well, well, really, I don't think I would be very entertaining at this point."

"Never mind. It's Christmas, and you've got to come over and talk to me."

With a despairing look around, he saw that no one would take his place. "Well, all right."

He stood up, and crossed over to her. Swaying, stiff-legged, as though balanced on golf sticks, he plucked at the cellophane wrap of a fresh pack of cigarettes. "How does one get these things open?" he mumbled.

"You're more nervous than I am!"

"I guess I probably am."

She thrust her surly face up at him. "Sit down. What's the matter? You're all pale and blotched. Have a little drink with me!"

"No, thank you very much." Declining the flask, he sank down into the chair beside her.

With a coarse grin, she breathed on him and asked: "Do you mind if I have another slug?"

"Not at all," he sighed, and lit his cigarette.

"I thought you might get embarrassed." She held up the flask and took a deep swallow. "Pah! That's what you need —change your mind?"

"No, thanks," sighed the man next to her, "I've seen too much of it."

"What!"

"Oh, I'm sorry," he answered in his well-bred accent. "I'm under a bit of a strain—"

"So am I," the woman said. "I always get drunk on Christmas. Thirty years ago exactly. My old man said: 'Go away. Don't bring your indecency back here, ever.' It was like the movies. It was even snowing."

"I'm very sorry to hear that."

"You needn't waste your sympathy. It happened thirty years ago." She looked at him with a crooked smile. "You keep shifting around. Why are you so nervous?"

He craned his neck and grimaced. "You see . . ." He regarded her coarse face doubtfully, and then seemed to give up caring whether she understood or not. "You're not the only one with problems. You'd be nervous too if you had just put your wife in a mental institution."

"No!" she drew back from him. "Poor dear. On Christmas Day!"

"Yes. Christmas Day."

George Pectin leaned closer to hear what would come next. The Chinese seemed not to have heard anything. The Hungarians nodded with their eyes closed, and the sailor pulled down a dixie cup at the water cooler. George heard the unhappy man say:

"Therefore, you can understand why I'm not very talkative."

The woman had continued to examine him from a distance. Her heavy red face had taken on a dowager's expression. "Why did you let them put her away?" she asked.

"*Let* them?" he said, twisting in his chair and turning his anguish full on her. "I had to recommend that she be committed."

"You committed your wife!"

"My God, I had to!" he said. "It was nothing I could help or prevent! She was—"

"Couldn't you help her?"

"Everything was tried. You can believe that. Her condition was progressive, and in the end she lost contact with reality."

"You mean she couldn't recognize you?"

"Sometimes not."

"The poor thing didn't recognize you today when you put her in?"

"Oh!" he said. "Please, if you don't mind."

She softened toward him, and murmuring "Poor dear!" patted his sleeve with her chapped and stubby hand. "Sure you won't have one?" she asked, drawing the flask from her handbag.

"Thank you, no." He peered out of the window, saying: "I think we're in New York State now. That was either Greenwich or Rye back there."

She took a deep pull from the flask and retained it in her hand.

"Couldn't your wife have done something creative?"

Wearily he turned his attention from the window. "Creativity wasn't the problem."

"It's a way of passing the time though." The woman stared ahead with bright eyes. Her speech was thickening. "Wherever I go I look at people and think about them, and imagine who they are. Then when I go home, and I'm boozed up, I can bring all their faces before me like playing cards, and I think about them like friends or acquaintances. Isn't that creative?"

"Well," he said, "it would depend on the point of view. I suppose one could call it that."

Lurching past a complex of factories, the train moved more quickly toward New York. George Pectin watched the familiar Lifesaver factory flash by. One of the Hungarians pointed to it and explained something to the other. The sailor was asleep. The Chinese were now listening to the man and woman without seeming to.

"I'm twenty-four hours late," she said.

"I beg your pardon?"

"Twenty-four hours. I was supposed to get to Jersey City last night and spend Christmas with some of my relatives, but I didn't get there. It's happened before too. I never seem to get there."

"Never arrive at the house of your relatives?" the exhausted man beside her inquired, with a show of interest.

"Something always happens. Last night in Stamford—"

"Of course, it's perfectly understandable," he said in a stronger tone. "Does this only happen with your relatives?"

"Yes, it's always something."

"The probability is that you are still afraid to face them because of what happened thirty years ago. Even though these people have obviously forgiven whatever it was—are they your father's people?"

"Yes," the woman replied, lifting her strong face to look at him. "What of it?"

"There, you see!" he exclaimed, with rising authority and triumph. "Your feeling of guilt is perfectly natural. It's responsible for the drinking too, in all likelihood."

(*87*

She studied him with disbelief.

He said: "By this time you must have realized that I am a psychiatrist."

The conductor came down the line collecting all tickets. After he had gone by, she said to the man with cigarette smoke obscuring his face: "You're a doctor!"

"Yes, I am."

"And you didn't help her?"

"I couldn't. . . ."

"Physician, heal thyself!"

"It wasn't possible for me to treat my wife. Don't you understand? It would be contrary to medical ethics. I turned her over to one of my colleagues.

"That's peculiar," the woman said.

"It's done frequently." The doctor turned sorrowfully from her, and the blotches stood out on his cheeks. Gazing around him, he encountered the wide-open eyes of Hungarians, Chinese, and sailor, and George Pectin's ear was a few yards away.

She caught his arm, and said: "You can help other people, but you can't help yourself."

"Perhaps. You may have a point there."

Clutching the flask, the woman got unsteadily to her feet and demanded of him: "Did you ever stop to think that maybe you brought your patients' troubles home to your wife, and that's why—"

"No, no!" he waved at her. "It was an endocrine imbalance. The endocrines . . . there's no use in trying to—

can you guess what I'm talking about. It's a chemical process. Irreversible."

His interrogator said unexpectedly: "You mean there's
something organically wrong with her?"

"Exactly."

"The poor dear! Would she recognize you now?"

"I suppose so."

"Don't you want her to get out?" the woman asked,
bringing her eyes close to his.

"Of course I do. But it's impossible."

"Not with faith?" she asked.

He stood up and made an attempt to brush the cigarette
ashes from his clothes. "No, absolutely not."

"Then the truth is," she said, wavering before him, "in
your heart, you don't want to get her out."

The doctor bowed ludicrously, almost losing his balance.
"I must tell you," he said, "we'll have to drop it now. Our
conversation. Frankly, I've been hoping for a holiday.
Now I find it's turning into a busman's holiday. Shall we
drop it, if you don't mind? Do you see the lights on the
clover leaf? We're getting near New York. I must collect
my baggage. Sorry I won't be able to help with whatever
you may have brought along. Goodbye then."

He made his way to the luggage rack and took down the
heavy suitcases. Then, as the Chinese and Hungarians, and
the sailor and George Pectin, watched, and the woman held
out her silver-plated flask and beckoned, he took down the
golf bag and propped it behind him.

He shook his head, refusing to sit down again. The woman gestured toward him, smiling and offering the flask. He kept shaking his head, and fumbled for a cigarette. The pack of Kents escaped him. It fell to the floor, and as he went after the package his golf bag toppled and crashed to the floor of the train. Loose golf clubs slid along the aisle. He pursued them, going down on his knees with the comical anguish that wouldn't let him go.

The Chinese boy handed him several clubs. He accepted them, stammering: "Please don't help me!"

Getting up, he opened the compressed-air door and carried the golf bag out to the platform between the cars. He returned to struggle with the suitcases, got the door open again, and paused, looking back at the woman with his foolish smile. "Well, merry Christmas!" he said. The door hissed twice and closed behind him.

« 9 »

Hallucinations

A RIBBON OF SNOW leaped outside the train window. It ran up to the suspension bridge, and all at once spread out, covering the ice on the river. Buoys and markers stuck up above the blinding surface. George Pectin put on his shades, and felt better. He had brought Polaroid glasses to hide his tears. After the deserted boat yard, all signs of the river vanished. Fir trees rushed by. The snowy morning turned cool green. The irregular streak ran by the roadbed again, and he turned back to say:

"That's why I'm going ahead with it. I'll fly to Juarez in

April—after she's out and I've got her settled. It's better to do it in Mexico. You don't need harsh grounds for divorce there. Only incompatibility."

"That right?" the one beside him murmured.

"All the same it's a shock, I imagine. Beginning today . . . the worst part: 'You don't love me any more?' 'I'm sorry, honey, I don't.' I just couldn't make that. So I wrote her a letter, to precede my visit. The coward's way, perhaps. Cutting off the dog's tail by inches, as my mother used to say. But it's not so easy to be courageous when you're about to injure a fine woman. A beautiful person really. Not to mention my son. He's five. I'll have to go down to Tennessee and pick him up."

"That right?"

"The point is, this afternoon . . . how can I explain it to her? When love has gone, what can you do? You can't legislate it back. It's impossible to get the vote out. One votes with the penis finally."

"Pardon?"

"I'm sorry! It's inconsiderate of me to think out loud," George Pectin said. Behind the dark glasses he peered anxiously at the man beside him. He was big and heavy, and wearing Polaroids too. The two men looked at one another. We can't see each other at all, George Pectin marveled. We never will.

The thought pleased him, and he went on: "A friend of mine is Russian. She says that the peasants conceive of the male organ as a rock-headed muzhik. 'Durak,' he is, and our organ too. It's stubborn, only does what it wants, and not necessarily what you think it should do. Can't learn anything, can't be reasoned with, makes the same mistake over and over, yet we follow Durak. But also, where it refuses to go, we can't go either. It happens that my Durak seeks danger and destruction, and shies away from all that's good and wholesome in a woman. So I have to get a divorce. Follow the peasant dictator until he gets tired of the game. If you have an obsession, the only thing to do is take it all the way. Don't you think?"

His fellow-rider made a noncommittal gesture.

"It may be that I want to destroy myself. At least temporarily. Well, now is the time, while I'm young enough. Get it over with. A few months ago," George Pectin laughed, "I was in this obscure bar, terribly drunk and by myself. I'm a professional, and don't often get that way. There was this hat-check girl, lean and hostile, with bangles on her arms. She looked like a member of an Amazon guard. A terrible, sensual desire came over me to be humiliated or disgraced. Throw away my money. Fold towels in a whorehouse. Anything. I told her so. She looked at me, and said: 'You're not my type.' Later I saw her kissing another woman. . . ."

George Pectin gazed out the train window at the factories of West Haven. "Why do you suppose a man wants to be destroyed?" he asked.

"Beats me."

"There has to be a reason. Do you think it's a peculiarly Christian illness? The idea of guilt. A two-thousand-year-old crime against humanity—"

"New Haven!"

"I get off here." The man wearing Polaroids stretched and yawned.

"It's funny," George Pectin said. "In the last two or three years, passing through New Haven, a number of people asked what I was studying at Yale. They must have taken me for a graduate student."

"That so?"

"In Old Saybrook once I was refused service in a liquor store, because I didn't have a card to prove I was of age. But that happened ten years ago."

"God ... when I mentioned Juarez you should have seen the anguish in her face. It was like clubbing a deer."

"Sorry, I don't believe in what you're doing."

"Who *does?* Who 'believes in' divorce, abortion, or any of those things? ..."

He smoked until his throat was raw; his face reflected in the dark windowpane had a sickly hue. Glancing across the aisle of the smoking car, he saw a young, ruddy priest. The man's powerful red hands were clasped about his Bible. He would open the Bible and read a little, and then lift up his head as if to think over and savor the passages. He had the noblest expression George had ever seen on a young man's face.

If he could approach the rugged priest, and perhaps gain some consolation from him ... But there would be no point in it. The priest would automatically disapprove of the divorce, and they would have nothing to talk about. Shortly after this, as a silvery lake moved by, he had his hallucination.

The woods came to an abrupt end, and the train rolled past a drive-in movie theater. Once in summer George had been startled to see the lunatic image of Jerry Lewis capering over the housetops of a nearby suburban development. The hallucination was that now, in the dead of winter when the drive-in movie was not operating, he saw Jerry Lewis again, leaning over the houses and beckoning to him.

THE LAWYER IN THE SMALL Connecticut town had looked him over sadly.

"Are you sure you want to do this?"

"Yes, sir," he replied. "It's the best thing."

"Hasn't she been a good wife to you?"

"Yes, she was," George Pectin said. "But we can't go on, and that's all there is to it."

On Sunday morning he had walked through the village in which he hoped Mary would settle. The inn would make a fine temporary lodging, only a block from school. He lingered by an old quarry watching some boys Davey's age play out a Western scene, using an abandoned car as a stagecoach.

Beyond a small hill the Connecticut River flowed into Long Island Sound. Bright mists sparkled on the river, and out at sea. Tankers plied the sound. The river current, with a tremendously broad and powerful flow, was bringing ice cakes down to the open water.

He had paused at the Village Green by the old black cannon with its little pyramid of balls. The people of the town moved among the churches. A foghorn and church organ were dismally synchronized, making him shiver, and an electronic carillon started up with a terrible jangle.

Now, on the train back to New York, with the town receding, he closed his eyes, recalling the night before. Not being able to sleep, he tiptoed down the carpeted stairs of the old inn, and set out along a dark, empty street. There was no moon, only an occasional street light. Patches of snow seemed oddly luminous. Presently the sidewalk ended. Far behind him the church clock struck one, and he listened to his own footsteps. The black-top road wound past a brook. He ran his hand along the railing of an old wooden bridge. In the distance he made out the waters of Long Island Sound, and again became aware of the hoarse horn and faintly clanging bell. Great shadowy houses lay deep in the woods.

All at once he heard a voice call out his first name. George Pectin stopped in the middle of the road. The voice he heard came from the woods, and he followed it, and heard his name again. A darkened house loomed near, at the end of a gravel driveway, but whoever was calling him must, he knew, be waiting among the trees. He found himself at the edge of the woods, listening.

"Yes!" he shouted. "Who is it?"

He heard a cough that might have come from a sleeper in

the house, but no other sound. Still he felt a presence in the woods luring him on, a gleaming black movement behind a pale twig, like a cigarette. George shivered in the cool, salty night. He stepped backward slowly to the road. Sweating, he walked slowly away from the spot, looking back over his shoulder until he reached the bridge. Approaching car headlights were a relief. The car swept past him, illuminating far ahead the torch on the Village Green. He was not so far from town after all, and hurried back to safety.

Sergeant Pectin had lain in the oxygen tent with lobar pneumonia. His lungs were filling up. A lazy master sergeant carried him dead on the morning report. Dreary Alaskan suns filtered into his room. Faintly over the Armed Forces Radio he heard Nat Cole singing "Sweet Lorraine." White, shadowy nurses and medical technicians passed before his window. He tapped on the isinglass to catch their attention. He was enveloped in fire, but the pure oxygen was as delicious as spun candy. Somebody poured cool alcohol on his back, and rubbed it in. The thermometer was under his armpit again. A nurse bent down, and smiled through the window. The chaplain came, and George refused him. It was night again. Flames danced in his head. The breathing space remaining to him was smaller and thicker.

Then, in the dark outside his tent, a figure emerged. George Pectin would never forget him. He stepped out of the fever and sat down just outside his tent, as clearly and boldly outlined as all the other figures, the nurses and hospital attendants, were dim and fleeting. It was a cool, supercilious young man, who sat with his legs negligently crossed. He had a smooth sweep of blond hair. He was dressed in a dinner jacket and black tie, and carried a gleaming black Ronson lighter case. The young man kept tapping his unlit cigarette against the black case in a most irritating and insulting manner.

He announced in an offhand way that his name was Alaric. He had come to inform Sergeant Pectin that his life story, containing the most intimate and personal details, had been sold by Mary Pectin to the *New York Daily Mirror*. It would be called "The Confessions of a Pneumoniac." Mary had no choice, being short of money. But she was also naïve and trustful, and told far more than necessary. Alaric had been able to extract many secret details from her—what George liked to do in bed, and so on. All of these would be in the *Daily Mirror* series. Smiling, tapping his cigarette against the black case, the suave young visitor wanted George to know there was nothing he could do about his impending exposure. Sergeant Pectin whispered silently: "Why are you doing this to me?" and Alaric lit up the cigarette and laughed.

Sergeant Pectin began to cough. The nurse came in, and Alaric withdrew but did not go away. His ironical smile waited in the corner of the room. George signaled the nurse, begging her to crank the bed down where it bulged under the back of his knees. It was cutting down the circulation, and unless something was done about it he would die. In some way Alaric had been responsible for this. Now the menacing young man was fading, with a last derisive puff of smoke. The nurse cranked George's legs down. He was in flames again, but with a difference. Under the 105° fever, a tiny corner of intelligence remained. He could think and calculate, and fixed on one passing fragment of truth: that with great calm he must breathe lightly, and with little shallow breaths, within the inch allotted to him, and if he did this he would get through the night. There was a sting in his shoulder. Five hours later he woke up clear-headed with his temperature down to normal. But still he believed that Alaric had been with him, and asked the chaplain to call New York and stop the *Daily Mirror* series while there was time.

RAILROAD TRACKS WERE SPREADING OUT over the Bronx. A red sunset covered New York. The Empire State Building was enveloped in smog and flames, and dark smudges hung solidly in the sky above Harlem.

A peculiar thing was happening to George Pectin. It was not new with him. Through the years he had grown accustomed to it happening at odd times, for no apparent reason. He was beginning to get an erection. Nothing in particular had excited him that he knew of. It happened independently. The detached sexual relation usually came when he was physically exhausted or at rest, not doing or thinking anything.

He had experienced it early in the morning on guard duty in Alaska. His company had crouched all night anticipating a simulated attack-exercise to be carried out by an infantry unit based a few miles away. The attack hadn't come that night after all. The dawn brought a waist-high ground fog. He couldn't see below his waist, but felt the wave of desire taking possession of him, remaining strangely independent, having, it seemed, a life of its own. After his return to civilian life the same thing happened quite often—late at night typing against a deadline, at the end of a long drive, or during a prolonged editorial conference.

Perhaps the movement of the train brought it on, but motion wasn't necessary. He had felt it again last week in his own office. From the thirtieth floor of the *Forecast* Building he gazed out over the Hudson at another red, smoky sundown. A pretty young staff reporter hired only a month before insisted on having his opinion of her first story. She invaded his contemplation and thrust the piece on him. So consumed was she by the prospect of success that no attention was paid to him as a man. She leaned on him; he smelled the clean, perfume-free ambitious body. She didn't want him but only his attention. Thus, they appeared to cling together; the girl clasping the man, looking over his shoulder, with her forefinger thrusting past his nose and touching her paragraphs; the man, brooding, exhausted, bored, with an aimless, gloomy sensuality rising in his trousers.

"One Hundred and Twenty-fifth Street!"

« 10 »

True Love

"NOWADAYS PEOPLE ARE QUESTIONING the entire institution of marriage, and all it stands for," George Pectin said to the man riding in the seat next to him. "I don't agree. All marriage means is permanently living together, supposedly in a joyful state. That has to be mastered like anything else. But not by vows, in my opinion. They just don't hold any more. What I'm getting at is this: assuming marriage for love, can the enchantment boy and girl feel in the beginning be maintained by an *act of will?* Eh? What do you think? Does it have to fade?"

The pale, angular face of his traveling companion was averted from him. The man cleared his throat and continued looking out the window. A faint spread of green covered a passing hillock.

"I realize . . ." George murmured. "It's probably . . . not your kind of subject."

The man had identified himself as an income tax collector. He announced his calling serenely, as though he had long since become resigned to hostile responses.

"I mean, even though marriage to one woman per lifetime can be *taxing*," George grinned, he knew, foolishly. A silence followed, and two long warnings came from the diesel horn.

"One trouble is, committing ourselves too early instead of searching until we find exactly the partner intended for us. That search takes courage, and skill too. Possibly computers can help. And there's been a suggestion—I think from Sweden—that everybody register his preferences, even perversions, with a government sexual agency. Then they could be run through a computer and matched up. There would be municipal sexual matching offices. Go down to City Hall not to get married but to find your natural partner on file. It could be handled by the unemployment people. Come to think of it, why not match up people with preferences that blend together? I have all kinds of urges, and I know I'd be a better person if I could act them out under the proper auspices."

At this the man turned and studied George with a tolerant smile.

"Please excuse me," George Pectin said. "I'm about to get divorced, and . . . Look at all these young couples getting on the train with pussywillows. Young people hand in hand. You can tell they've got hold of a beautiful mystery. But how long will they keep it? You and I know. Or perhaps we don't. Speaking for myself, it's occurred to me that except for the night we walked home together in the snow, and a few other nights, I'm not sure if I've ever known what love is. Something has been withheld from me. I'm speaking of true love. Yes, I know. *It fades*, supposedly. But I refuse to believe that I've been left out emotionally. I think it's just because I haven't met *her*.

> "Will I ever find
> The girl on my mind
> The one who is my ideal . . . ?"

"You think there's only one?" The tax collector gave a short laugh.

"No, obviously love takes all forms—as many as there are people. But I suspect that it has a single essence. We attain to this knowledge when we 'fall in love,' and it transfigures us. As you probably know, there's nothing in life to compare with the experience. But it dies. *It dies*, we are told, and there's no way to avoid the deterioration. *Housekeeping destroys love*. The beautiful mysteries of courtship have to fade (they tell us). Over the years the loved one must, as if according to natural law, turn into 'the old lady,' 'the ball and chain,' et cetera. Love itself becomes a laughingstock, a silly little prelude to procreation. Forget it. Grow up. Mature! (We are told)."

The tax collector watched Westport go by, and said: "The kids sort of get in the way, don't they?"

"To hell with them then! With all the pills now we don't *have* to have children!" cried George Pectin, adding hurriedly: "Of course, I love my son."

"Love is a leaky boat." The man beside him smiled. "You've got to keep bailing."

"Oh, very good. Be realistic. That's what they tell us. But I don't propose to let them get away with that line any longer. Am I divorcing a fine woman for nothing? No, I have the courage, even let's say the enterprise, to divorce her because I'm convinced, I have faith, that there's some- one else waiting for me. My feminine *double*. Most of us lack the guts to keep on searching for our counterpart. That's why there are so few happy marriages. We *settle*, and—"

"Yes, settle down," the man drawled out of his discon- certing, and also limiting, middle-class manliness. "First have your good time. Then start the family, and that part is over with. It's the law of nature—"

"Rise above natural law! . . ."

In a kindly tone, the other man said: "If you don't mind my saying so, I think you're—"

"A madman," said George Pectin cheerfully. "Of course, you would think that. I don't blame you. You're not the first, by any means. Around the magazine they're whispering: 'Pectin's cracked up.' It's all right. They're

stuck with what they have, and resent anybody else trying."

He wanted so much to inspire this practical man, win
him over, make him see that there was more to life than
accepting (with cheap wisdom) its unfair conditions.

"Grace," he said. "Grace is what we lose when love
starts to fade. The grace of being young with her when she
is young. The only children alive, giggling together in a
huge bed, sharing the secret, *cheating everybody*. . . . Can't
you remember? Why give that up so easily? Why give it
up at all? Refuse to let love slip. Make it stand up day after
day, until the years are dragged out of you. Resist even
then. Make the enchantment last. *Force* it to.

"I may not look it, but I'm forty-three. It's got to happen now. Sometimes I think of her as a cheerleader, or one
of those majorettes you see between the halves on television. Or a cool woman doctor, French, about thirty-five; a
German pianist with big, creamy shoulders. The divorced
wife of a Swedish diplomat!

"Don't you understand! It's agony to think that by a
fluke she may be in the seat behind me, or down the
aisle waiting for somebody to help her with her suitcase,
and a sailor will do it. Time is so short now. I can't bear to
stay on this shuttle of nothing happening. If I don't find
her . . . but I know I will. That's the easy part. The thing
after that will be how to keep the mystery between us
intact year after year."

The man beside him was speaking. The words came

fervently, and George was astonished by the emotional conviction behind them.

"Just love them," the tax collector said. "There's no use telling the truth. No use arguing with a woman. It just won't work. You can't treat them as an equal. Praise them. Tell them how beautiful they are. Tell them that they're right. For your own sake. Otherwise the argument will never end."

"But you're talking about *tactics*."

"You look at the one you married," the tax collector said. "The woman across the room, sitting there. The one you courted has gone. For you. But other people can see her. They can see what made you love her. Well, you can bring her back occasionally. It's hard, but you can."

"You're making it a chore, a duty," George Pectin broke in.

The other man smiled. "Of course, it's hard to love them when you're annoyed. You don't even like them. That's the hardest time—but for your sake, you've got to."

"Why, *why?*" George Pectin said angrily. "You talk like the most commonplace marriage manual. What kind of a life is that?"

"Mine," the tax collector said. "Yours too."

« *11* »

Carrousel

GEORGE HAD PROMISED to take the train, not fly, going down and coming back from Tennessee. He obeyed Mary's every spoken wish except one. The flight to Juarez was already booked, and he would have to go through with it. In every other way he was her servant, fetching and carrying, helping as best he could to convert two rooms in the Connecticut inn into a new home for his wife and son.

Throughout the afternoon he hardly dared look at her—only to remark that she appeared to be a bit short of breath, though otherwise fresh and healthy-looking, with a good color. He kept bidding Mary to sit and rest and not tire herself, once even assisting her into a chair. But finally, leaving her among the newly opened boxes and suitcases, George Pectin took off.

NEXT DAY HE TELEPHONED ahead from the club car, to give Davey a surprise.

"I'm *on the train* . . . coming down to get you. Right now! Well . . . there's a farm. I can see horses and chickens, and a field of cows. All the hillsides are covered with dandelions!"

Approaching Washington, the train slowed. For a mile it crawled silently. George imagined all the trains being drawn into the center of the city by magnet. But there had been that nightmare years ago when a red-eyed locomotive burst into the Washington railroad station and kept on going, trumpeting like a mastodon, and scattered the screaming people. There must have been a moment of horror and at the same time a kind of ecstasy for the engineer, George had always thought. With no help for it, all control gone, he might have howled as his diesel went smashing through the terminal.

George Pectin never could sleep on trains. At this Virginia junction where they changed locomotives in the night, it would have been impossible even for a good sleeper. There was always the unnecessary shouting and swinging of lanterns, endless banging around, the hauls and jolts, the train gently rolling backward to a stop, resting in silence somewhere; then, it seemed to the passenger lying in his berth, senselessly being propelled forward again, and coming to rest in another remote part of the yard.

His last visit had been in September. No one knew when Mary would be coming out. The little boy hadn't forgotten his mother, but she was somebody who wrote loving notes his aunt read to him. A thin, tired man with a gray face arrived and knelt before him, holding out his arms. He smoked cigarettes all the time. They played games, and the man tucked him in bed and kissed him, and promised that he would be home soon. Although he didn't say so, he wasn't sure that he wanted to go. Then Dad got back on the train again, coughed and put on dark glasses, and waved goodbye from behind a dirty window.

Three hours earlier they had been walking along a hillside. George was tired. His sister's family had gone on a picnic. He wandered about with his son. They had made desultory attempts to fly a kite, but the wind was uncertain. The kite would bob over their heads, and then come down. Now they walked hand in hand through the hot Sunday afternoon, and lay down on the grass. There was a game of knocking off each other's dandelion heads. Thirsty for a beer, George Pectin was about to suggest going back to the house.

He heard a bell tinkling. A bright-red wagon was moving slowly up the valley road. The bell tinkled, and he heard faint cries from the houses along the route. Davey looked at his father expectantly.

The carrousel man also sold ice cream. George dropped a shining fifty-cent piece in his son's palm, and said: "Go on! Run!" Everywhere children were running out of the hills. They came from behind trees, leaping over fences, and racing across the road. A horde of small blue jeans and white dresses converged on the wagon.

The tiny carrousel was mounted on a trailer behind the ice cream wagon. A cage protected the children from falling out. The music started, and the hurdy-gurdy sound echoed in the valley. George Pectin drew near, holding the red box kite he had bought in New York, and saw his son astride a miniature horse. He was gazing about him with a beatific smile, holding an ice cream cone. The little boy caught sight of him and waved. All the children were going around, and every few seconds behind the cage Davey's face whirled past him.

The twanging, jangling melody reproached him:

> . . . Why can't I free your doubtful mind,
> and melt your cold, cold heart?

He didn't have a cold heart. The children were clustered together on benches in a pine grove. Davey said something to a few of them, and they turned to look at him. George Pectin smiled back. But holding the kite he felt citified and unimpressive. Calling to Davey, he began to run. He ran on the hillside, paying out the kite string behind him. He was no Pied Piper. Nobody followed him. Davey's Pa from New York was alone on the hillside, running, in gray slacks, with his Dacron jacket flapping, while the children looked on in wonder. He ran over the hills of Tennessee with a kite that wouldn't fly. Once it got stuck in the branches of a sycamore. He shinnied up and got it, and in one continuous action came down and went on leaping along the hillside.

He ran over the hill and back, and along the top, and down again, with the red box kite bobbing behind him, now bouncing off the grass, lifting up a little and dropping. Sweat poured over him. It filled his eyes so that he couldn't see, and he sank to the ground. He had run in circles and was back where he started, with the kite lying beside him. A short distance away stood a pair of little legs in shorts. His son was regarding him brightly over the top of his second ice cream cone.

THE LITTLE BOY SAT CROSS-LEGGED on the hooked rug while the toy train chugged in circles around him. It gave off puffs of smoke, and whistled when you wanted it to. Every once in a while he would throw a switch; the train would stop. He could make it back up and go forward, and stop again; attach freight cars to it, then take them off; position plaster tunnels over the track and remove them, arrange lead soldiers in formation on the bridge, so that they would appear to be marching out of the yard; start the train, stop it, knock the soldiers down with marbles.

The train was Mary's homecoming surprise. George Pectin patiently helped Davey put it all together, but he had a theory. It was that children didn't really enjoy toy trains. On the contrary, the trains made them nervous. After the first hour or so of starting and stopping, putting on more cars, and throwing switches, they became fretful. At this point they began to take pleasure in derailing the engine. They would make the locomotive go too fast, throw the switch, and laugh at the ensuing wreck, crowing with delight over the mess, freight cars and caboose lying on their sides, wheels turning slowly. . . . Children always did this, he had noted, and his five-year-old was no exception. Davey became cranky and threw marbles. With relief George dismantled the railroad, hoping never to see it again.

"We haven't had too much sleep. Would you like to rest, Davey?"

"No."

His wife was brimming over with happiness. She didn't seem worried about the divorce any more. Where do I fit in? George Pectin thought, even though he was going to be free and didn't want to fit in.

Mary said vaguely: "Was it a nice trip back?"

The question unnerved him a little. Now that her son was home, she made conversation with the departing man.

"It was all right, but neither of us got any rest to speak of. That's natural. He was excited. Weren't you, honey, coming home again?"

"Yes."

"*Did* you tell Janet how grateful—"

"She wasn't there. She's visiting my grandfather."

"I'll write her. Tomorrow, after we're settled in. . . ."

"I suppose," George Pectin said, with a glance at his son, who was arranging a pattern of marbles, "there's no point in saying anything yet."

"Oh, no."

"Besides, I'll be down regularly."

"Yes, please. That would be good."

"The thing is to establish a regular rhythm of visiting. Children like to be able to count on things happening regularly. That's why we're a bit n-e-r-v-o-u-s at the moment."

"It will pass," she murmured serenely.

I ALWAYS SEEM TO BE BEHIND a window, George Pectin thought angrily. His wife and son watched him from the station platform. They reminded him of a daguerreotype. Mary's hand rested on the boy's shoulder. They didn't move, and were simply looking at him. Davey's brown little face showed no emotion. He was now in the uniform of a navy officer, holding a toy aircraft carrier.

After the train pulled out it occurred to him why he had felt so uncomfortable in Mary's new home. It was antiseptically, depressingly clean and neat. For dust or the lack of it, he blamed her either way.

« *12* »

Split Screens

THE UNIFORMED VENDOR on the Boston-New York run wore several hats. Small and nervous, with a pinched face, he walked through the train calling out: "Cigarettes! Candy bars! Chewing gum!" A short time later he reappeared offering: "Milk! Orange juice! *Cau-ca-Cola!*" and finally: "Ma-ga-zines!" Following this he would sprawl out in the last car—in which George Pectin always rode if he could. Here the vendor would smoke and sleep until it was time to go through the cars again.

"You practically live on this train, don't you?" George
Pectin said. "I should think that sometimes it would be hard
to *place yourself*. When you get off, the ground must seem
unreal. And the changing seasons, as you go over this same
route day after day, could get to seem unreal, I'd imagine.
The scenery . . . the same tree, inlet, and pond; the same
rowboat half-sunk at the dock. . . . It could become like
walls to your life, or a painted backdrop on either side of
the train. Please understand, I'm not asking this out of mere
curiosity. I've been watching you for months—"

"Feast your eyes!" said the exhausted man, taking out a
cigarette.

"I'm not trying to probe. I was hoping that out of your
own experience you might help me understand something
about myself. What it is . . ." George Pectin frowned. "I
can't transpose environments."

"WHEN I WAS TWELVE, they sent me off to summer camp
in New Hampshire. I didn't like it . . . morning dips, calis-
thenics, campfires, sleeping outdoors, the rain falling on
your poncho, camp spirit. For the first two or three weeks
I felt displaced, as if the camp were a dream. I ran around,
made my bed, sang camp songs, completely separated from
all of it. When we played baseball, I felt separated from the
game. In school I was a pretty good first baseman. In camp
I couldn't catch a fly ball. It always fell yards away from
me. But I gradually accustomed myself to the camp dream,

and got inside of it. I learned to judge a fly ball, and things were easier.

"In the middle of the summer my father came in to see me. But now, you see, since I was used to camp, he was an outsider, and unreal. I couldn't accommodate myself to the idea that he had dropped in, practically from another planet, and inserted himself where his face simply didn't belong. I could hardly talk to him. There was a transparent wall between us. I must have acted strangely. He went away before the afternoon was half over.

"But when summer ended and camp was over, and we all got on the train, the train seemed to provide a legitimate passage between my camp world and home world. But there was one point when I felt that *the train was the only reality*. Do you ever feel that way?"

The candy butcher grunted and smoked.

"It's been that way all my life," George Pectin said. "Six years ago, for instance, I was on a train, going to visit my uncle. We were approaching the town he lived in. The conductor had opened the doors. I took down my suitcase and put on my hat and coat. The train began to slow down, and then it stopped in the open somewhere . . . just came to a halt about two miles from the station. Nobody explained anything. Probably another train coming through, I thought. We just sat there. I looked out the window at the long grass covering an embankment, a white fence, a big elm tree, and behind it a small meadow. It seemed familiar. I looked again. It was my uncle's house. I couldn't believe it. What was his house doing *there*, next to my train? Then

I realized that of course it was. I had often watched the trains go by from that meadow.

"I sat in the train and looked stupidly at my uncle's house. Very slowly it occurred to me that I could get off. Nobody was meeting me at the station. I could take my suitcase, get off the train, scramble up the embankment, and be at my uncle's house in one minute. I didn't *have* to go on with the train all the way to the station—then take a taxi back out here. But . . . because of whatever is wrong with me . . . I couldn't move. I felt paralyzed. It wasn't *scheduled* for me to leave the train here. I thought vaguely that the conductor would be disturbed and angry to find one of his passengers gone. He would see the ticket stub and no passenger. I thought I might write the conductor a note. But it was also against the rules to descend from the train before it reached its destination and stopped. It wasn't permitted. Here the train had come to rest in forbidden territory. The railroad couldn't be blamed if my uncle's house happened to be nearby . . . Then the train started up again, and it was too late.

"That's why it's been hard for me to *get off* anywhere," George Pectin said. "It's why I never finish anything. Success is a different scene from mine. It's out there, and I'm here behind my window. The idea of Success and I being in the same place isn't real. I'm stuck in the train. Do you see what I mean?"

The candy butcher was going through a series of gestures. His shoulders went up. He thrust his hands out, lifted his eyes to heaven, and made a sound like: "Ech!"

He got up, shouldering his basket, and started up the aisle.

"Cigarettes! Candy bars! Chewing gum!"

Did I put him off in some way? George Pectin wondered.

« *13* »

News from Cape Cod

HE FOUND A LETTER from his sister in the mail-box, and immediately opened it.

Dear Brother (Janet began), by now you must have collected David. Now that it's over I must admit that having him was something of an ordeal. But I was glad to help you, and we'll say no more about that.

She reported that their grandfather was failing badly. Dr. Sears explained that the old man was no longer rational during a great part of the day. His medical opinion had an edge of warning.

"Your grandfather has had a series of little strokes," he had told Janet. "Each one by itself doesn't mean too much, but cumulatively they weaken him and also tend to result in personality changes. Unfortunately, in my experience, psychic alterations produced by strokes are practically always what the rest of us would call 'bad.' The signs are familiar: erratic, whimsical behavior, morbid suspicions, often of the family, which get worse, and outbursts of hostility that seem to come for no reason at all. This, frankly, has happened with your grandfather. He's not the same person you knew. Also"—the doctor had paused and given Janet a meaningful look—"the present situation in his home encourages some of these symptoms."

What he had called "the present situation" involved Maria, the Italian housekeeper. She had taken charge of the household during their grandmother's last years, when Laurie had been in a virtual coma. All the family knew that Maria had insinuated herself into the old man's trust—it was feared legally as well as emotionally. Short, strong, and motherly, she had a sick husband in another town on the Cape and four teen-age daughters. On weekends she went home. The rest of the time she lived in the house with their grandfather, devoting herself to making his last years different from all the others that had preceded them.

I don't know how she does it (Janet wrote), but she has him wrapped around her little finger. For one thing, he's suspicious, as Dr. Sears mentioned, of every one of his relatives excepting Uncle Kenneth. He won't talk to Dougal and Jenny, or have them in the house. He barely tolerates Martha, Kitty and Tom. This will hurt your feelings, but I don't think he knows who you are. He has his doubts about me. At one point he walked in while I was sitting in the living room, and said: "No, we won't let you have your party on the lawn. Last year those blackguards trampled over the rose beds." He was speaking of the church fair, which hasn't been held on our grounds for twelve years. I don't know whether to be flattered or insulted . . . being mistaken for a church lady.

For some reason, his family means next to nothing to him now, and Maria grows dearer to his heart (Janet's letter continued). I wonder why this is. He was the pillar for so many years. Supporting most of us at one time or another. But do you suppose that subconsciously he always wanted to kick over the traces. I can't believe it. And yet the jolly Italian woman seems to give the dour Scot some kind of excitement that he never experienced before. Now, almost ninety . . . you'll find this hard to believe . . . he is crazy about pizza and hero sandwiches. An odd sight is to watch this stern idol of our youth tottering and bleary-eyed, drinking red wine and gobbling down pieces of salami popped into his mouth by his adoring Maria. As he eats this stuff, there appears on his face an expression of . . . I don't know . . . idiotic complacency.

And she takes him everywhere. Late in the winter they attended, of all things, an ice hockey game, the Bruins, in the Garden. He suffered a rather sizable stroke the next day, but then bounced back. She drives him to the beach. They sit in the car and look at the ocean. And then she takes him to huge Italian celebrations with her endless family, and you can imagine the rolls of spaghetti being shoveled down the old man's throat. Maria told me about this with great pride: how "your grandfather *danced!*" Danced? She must be trying to kill him. But when you think of it, what right have we to say anything? Have any of us volunteered to stay with him? Did *we* move into the ancestral home to comfort him during Laurie's last years? No, we were too busy. We had our own affairs. I don't say we should have interrupted our lives to maintain the death watch, but the fact is, we didn't. I forgot—one of us tried. Aunt Kitty. She spent three months taking care of her barely conscious mother and trying to preside over her father's house. It was the work of a heroine. She got nothing but insults for it. Uncle Kenneth had the brutish suggestion that she ought to remain with her parents indefinitely "in exchange for her board and room." As if an attractive fifty-two-year-old widow had no other prospects. And I'm sorry to say that Gramps treated her very roughly, evidently wanting a *new* experience with no family in it before he faded away . . . as he is now doing.

Finally a stranger had to come in and take charge, scold the cook and spy on the nurses. She took the trouble—admittedly, as we see it, with hope of gain—— to make friends with an irritable and irritating old man. She expended great amounts of her coarse feminine energy to corrupt him (if changing from Scottish to Italian culture at the age of eighty-seven represents corruption), to cheat him and indirectly us, steal from the house, which she does, and possibly by bringing him to Italian feasts and encouraging him to dance to hasten his death by a year. But then, when the end comes for him will we be able to complain? I wonder. Perhaps at the approach of ninety it's better to dance out of this life with your mouth full of pizza than lie in a room with the shades drawn, accepting tea and gruel from a starchy nurse.

Janet told of one amusing incident. Kenneth's daughter and her husband had not shown much interest in the head of the clan. Upon hearing of the stroke that followed the hockey game, they suddenly appeared in Cape Cod with an enormous vest of many colors, specifically the colors of Gramps's clan, his own tartan. Gramps was pleased with the vest and wore it all the time. But he immediately forgot who the donors were, and went around boasting: "See what my niece Eleanor gave me!" Kenneth's daughter received no credit for being thoughtful. To be fair, she had money and was not concerned with a financial reward. Even if she had been, that possibility was now out of the question. The family savings were almost gone. Round-the-clock nursing and other medical expenses had consumed tremendous amounts. The old man who had believed so devoutly in life insurance had cashed in nearly all of his policies to pay for death.

We are not going to get anything (Janet wrote). But why should we, really? There's one somber note. Many years ago he wrote a policy for Kitty. It's been paid up for years. Now he has asked her to sign it over to Maria. Out of pride, she will. The fool! Let

(*123*

me give you my last memory of Gramps. I don't think I'll see him alive again. It was midnight. I was watching a late movie on television. I heard him coming down the stairs. He was fully dressed! "Good morning!" he said cheerily. I tried very gently to prove to him that it was not morning. "Nonsense!" he said, looking out at the new moon. "It's a beautiful day. Let's go for a drive." What an agony it was to talk him out of it.

Speaking of agony, there was something that happened near the end of Kitty's stay. I wasn't going to mention it, but if you still have writing ambitions this is the sort of thing that may interest you. It was terribly undignified and horrible, and yet in a strange way touching. (Nothing *is* sacred, is it? Or perhaps everything is.) You know how Gramps refused to admit the existence of anything improper, especially in his house. To the end Laurie was his bride. Even when she sank into second childhood, and then infancy, he would not accept any suggestions that there was anything different about her. The terrible toil of the nurses, changing sheets two or three times a night. . . . He had nothing to do with that. He continued to sit and talk with her as always, taking no notice of the fact that she was far away from what he was saying.

Kitty stayed up with her mother for months, to save the expense of a night nurse, and this ordeal practically wrecked her—especially since Gramps turned on the television at top volume during the daylight hours. She simply didn't sleep for more than an hour or two at a time. Finally she said that for one night she would have to rest or collapse. A nurse would have to be sent for. He answered: "Nonsense," and declared that he would sit up, and would not be dissuaded. Early in the morning Kitty heard a commotion in the bedroom at the other end of the house. She got up to see what had happened, and found her father taking refuge in the bathroom. And her poor sweet mother was laughing and making pies in bed, and throwing them about. It was all over the wall, and she was gloriously happy as she had been nine decades before, and all the years between had fallen away.

I am sorry to describe this, even to you, yet not ashamed. When I'm testy and out of sorts, I remind myself that life begins and ends in a great pile of the stuff, and think: "Why not?" and somehow it makes me laugh and feel better.

P.S. I enclose a trivial but interesting document. When Kitty was watching at the bedside one night, our grandmother began to ramble in the tired, little-girl voice in which she spoke during the last year or two. This is what she said. Meanwhile, goodbye for now. Love, and a big kiss from the whole family.

George Pectin picked up the fragment Janet had enclosed. In his Aunt Kitty's blurred hand, it read:

I want to be buried in a brown cheesecake but not a curly ox tail. No it would never do to drink that. Ellen does not enter a room with any ease and we must have plenty of good hot rolls don't you think so? Oh dear what can the matter be Johnny's so long at . . . I'm afraid I'll take out all those black compartments no not compartments comparisons and follow them out. I don't want to take mine and I don't want to take ours but I guess they'll be all right. Don't paste in any quotations. Three jacks and a glass of chair and they made a cataplane out of it or what ever it is. And where do your feet go where the curlings are? It is good wholesome food and now I'll be up in a minute. There is nothing down to put up in. How are your flannels and that should be good for them, shouldn't it? Piggins don't grow, do they? Go to the wedding, go to the Christmas. One world foot, two feather girls foot, oh mercy, mercy me.

PART III « *Nowhere* »

« 14 »

_____

Flight to Juarez

THE JET FROM El Paso taxied slowly to a halt at
Kennedy Airport. It vibrated with the morning sun
ablaze on its wings, wheels touching the yellow blocks,
engines screaming. The men on the ground held their ears
until the scream died away; then the ramp locked, and a file
of passengers began coming out of the plane. A meek old
couple, two Navy officers, a mother with crying twins, an
executive with an attaché case and a topcoat folded over his
arm, passed by the stewardesses, one of whom was smiling,

and the other, a red-headed girl, actually laughing goodbye to them.

There was an interval before a youngish man with dark circles under his eyes emerged from the cabin. He paused in front of the laughing stewardess. "You might as well have this," he said. Thrusting a package into her arms, he hurried away without looking back.

THE TALL, BEARDED MAN moved about on his open-air terrace, thinking, with his hands clasped behind his back. Now and then he stopped to ponder the rooftops of Manhattan before resuming his purposeful tramp. A blue haze over Central Park took a moment of his attention. With a grunt he stooped to pick up a matchstick from the tile floor and dropped it over the railing. A little later he brought out a golden watering can and tended a row of potted plants. In shorts and an old sweat shirt, he resembled a comfortable philosopher of some kind.

George Pectin stood and watched him. "Sorry to drop in unannounced, Tor," he said. "It being Easter, I imagined that you might be relaxing. Lying out in the sun and having a glass of iced tea. Don't you ever let up? I just have to talk. You're the only ones I felt I could turn to."

The tall man went indoors. He came back rolling out a typewriter mounted on a large stand and placed it in the center of the terrace. A table, also on casters, followed. Notes and memoranda covered its broad surface, arranged in neat piles and weighted down by stones, and a box full of yellow typing paper and carbons was set alongside the machine.

"I wouldn't bother you except that . . . I absolutely need to talk."

Receiving no answer, George Pectin said: "But under the circumstances I guess I'd better leave."

At this the bearded man wagged his finger reprovingly.

"Oh, good. Well, if it's all right, Tor, I'll wait around for a bit." George sat down in a wicker chair.

Now his old friend, Torvald Smith, studied the horizon. Hands behind his back again, he circled the terrace with an increasingly heavy tread, frowning and thinking.

George Pectin burst out: "It's not that I mind your silence! I know the trick. You used it when you were on the magazine. Interviewing celebrities, embarrass them by saying nothing but 'Uh huh' and 'Uh,' to get them off balance so that they would pour out confessions. But don't try that on me. I want to confess anyway. Besides, you're always trying to *impress* me. Don't you think I'm aware that when you're walking around like that you're imitating Einstein in his garden? But, Tor, that shouldn't be necessary with friends. Classmates, on the same baseball team. Think of how many times we've gone drinking together. I *know* you, Tor."

Torvald Smith threw back his head, and gave a deep bass laugh. But, still thinking, he came to a stop in front of the typewriter.

"But I suppose we're enemies, in a way. You work so hard. Not only on your articles, and that Icelandic epic, or whatever it is. You work *people*," George Pectin told his old friend or enemy with growing irritation. "You try to work *me*. You're always *on*. Elaine has converted you from a jovial drinking companion into some sort of humorless prehistoric *mammoth*. Oh, I don't blame her. The whole thing has worked. The double egoism you people share that passes for love . . . maybe it is love . . . has made you revoltingly happy, and I might add, complacent. You haven't time for anyone. Together you're like twin barrels of a shotgun on a remorseless hunt for fame.

"You ought to see yourselves at a party . . . when there's some poor guest who, it has been decided, can do the Smiths some good. Heaven help him! He finds himself pinned on one side by two fishy eyes, and backed against the wall by that bully-beard of yours. You simply work him over, deprive the man of oxygen until he gives in. Well, you're not going to do that with me, Tor. You're not going to impress me one bit more than I intend to be impressed.

"Come off it, Tor. What's so earth-shaking that you're going to put through that typewriter? Your companion epic to the Saga of Grettir the Strong . . . something America really needs . . ." George Pectin crossed the terrace and peered at Torvald Smith's notes. "*The Ladies' Home Journal*. My god, you put a lot into it. But I guess that's why you're successful."

The door from the penthouse opened, and a young woman came out. Elaine Smith's movements were so lithe and quick that she seemed not to have occupied space between the door and the worktable. She had long hair, and gave the impression of swimming with her mouth a little open. George Pectin left them together and walked to the other end of the terrace.

The young woman spoke rapidly and the bearded man bowed his head in a deferential manner. When she had finished, he nodded and sat down. The door closed behind her. Furiously George Pectin watched Torvald Smith insert a sheet of yellow paper in the machine. Smith stared at it for several minutes, then with a growl struck the keys.

The typewriter leaped from the impact, as he pounded it without stopping. One page was finished, then several. A small mackerel cloud formation passed under the sun. Lights and shadows played on the terrace. Smith shuffled his notes, and typed on. With a quick slithering motion his wife was at his side again. She inspected what he had written, nodded, and caressed his big head before going back indoors. Hulking over the Smith-Corona, Torvald Smith redoubled his pace, and a spark flew out of the machine.

"I was divorced Friday. In Juarez," George Pectin said. He had been given a glass of iced tea, since Torvald Smith had now quit drinking.

"You were, eh?" Elaine said. She and her husband were scanning his first draft and making corrections.

"The flight isn't to Juarez, really. It's to El Paso. Then you cross the border. Establish residence in Mexico by staying over a day and a night. I went to Sylvia's Hotel."

"You've always wanted to, and now you did it, eh?"

"I haven't *always* wanted to, Elaine . . ."

"Now you can have another try at Gretchen," suggested his old friend.

"You insist on dignity for yourself—why not give it to others!" George Pectin flared. "Oh, I know there's a bit of Hagen in you, Tor. Siegfried's betrayer. A hint of the black forest. Brute of the North. I wouldn't want to have you as my block captain in bad times."

Again Torvald Smith roared with laughter. "I just don't want you to be the *only* man who never made it with her."

"There must have been others who didn't," muttered George Pectin.

"No." Smith shook his head. "Not one."

"I might. Because you introduced me to her after having your own affair, when you were interested in such things, you get a kick out of my—"

"Never mind," said Elaine Smith. "Let's hear about Pectin's divorce."

"Sometimes I think that guilt is my strongest emotion," George Pectin explained. "Try to believe this. From the beginning I was absolutely sure that the jet was going to crash. *Sure* of it. Strapped in my chair, terrified."

"Hmm? Right back to the primitive, eh?"

"Primitive is right. How close it is to the surface! I'm a reasonably sophisticated man, by all standards. But here I was, convinced that I would be struck down by *aesthetic retribution*, or you might say, the fitness of things. It was aesthetically appropriate for a man like myself who was divorcing his wife really without proper cause, and who had generally speaking messed up his early promise, to crash in flames."

"I think you might change 'nearly' to 'almost,'" said Elaine Smith to her husband.

"Right, darling."

"They were playing soft music at boarding time. It was so unreal. I remember this same lullaby coming out of the walls of the dental surgeon's office when I had a wisdom tooth extracted. It was a dream again—but I'd never emerge from this airborne thing. Don't tell me how foolish it was!" George Pectin said, as Elaine was about to speak. "I was perfectly aware, even at the time, that when a man feels guilty about mistreating someone he ought to love, he arranges his history in *destructive patterns*, so that the only logical outcome is his own death. I knew it was lunacy. But lunacy in this one instance was also going to be fact. The plane was going to crash, I knew, en route to Juarez or on the way home."

"I would take out the Freudian explanation of why Grettir set the fires," Elaine Smith said, crossing out a paragraph. "It isn't necessary in this context."

"It's run like a military operation!" Pectin laughed unhappily. He unfolded a paper and read aloud from the typewritten paragraph:

"You will board Flight 315 to El Paso. Upon arrival you will be met by Señora Rincon who will conduct you to Sylvia's Hotel in Ciudad Juarez. On the following morning, or in the afternoon, you will be taken to the office of your lawyer in Mexico, Lic. Rafael Vegas. Señor Vegas will proceed your documents and accompany you to court where, after you have signed the register, your divorce will be granted. Late in the afternoon (see your ticket) you will board the return flight to New York, arriving about 10 a.m. at John F. Kennedy International Airport."

"Who's your lawyer?" Torvald Smith joked, hastily reaching for his wife's hand.

"Daniel Elgin, Park Row," George Pectin said. "Frankly, I don't see anything funny about it. These instructions, in my opinion, are chilling. How matter-of-factly lawyers go about separating people!"

"You wanted a divorce, didn't you?" said Torvald Smith, after making a note.

"At Kennedy, taking off, you wouldn't believe it. I was scared to death. Trembling. . . . An old woman was in the chair beside me, next to the window. A Catholic. She opened her prayer book. When we went down the runway she was praying like mad to her saint and fingering a cross. The ignorance and superstition involved annoyed me so that I forgot to be afraid, and we were in the air, above the clouds before I knew it.

"The stewardess was a pretty little redhead with those precise military shoulders I like. The kind I dream of as rescuing me—but that's something else. I found that I was adoring her, and using her beautiful competence as a shield against my panic. It was the worst kind of guilt-panic, Tor.

Please don't look so complacently at me. Fear comes in waves. I was terrified that the plane would fold up, as if on hinges, and slowly come apart. I had chosen the aisle seat so that just as the plane started to break in two I would be able to jump to the section that gave the greater promise of being able to fly a little. I had carefully avoided the chair by the window, and let the old woman have it, because if the side wall fell away the person in that seat would topple into space without a prayer. Do you understand me?"

"You were scared."

"Oh, hell, Tor," George Pectin said in a hurt tone. "I've flown a lot. This was a phenomenon. After all, I didn't invent myself. Something produced the kind of person I represent. The interesting thing is, here is Modern Man about to be divorced, trying to please what he—on a primitive level—considers God's aesthetic sense.

"In other words, my unconscious hope was that if I could manage *really* to believe in my imminent death—if the divorce cost me enough, in terms of suffering—it might then seem aesthetically appropriate for the sufferer to live!"

"That *is* interesting," Elaine Smith said in a low voice to her husband, and she looked at George Pectin, beginning to make notes.

"I know it will seem ridiculous," Pectin went on, his eyes shining, "but during these moments of torment I gradually began to fall in love with the stewardess. The way she worked the aisle; her beautiful shoulders, competence and bravery. She smiled at me twice. She was like a mistress, virgin and angel of mercy in one—flirtatious and radiant, and I loved her. When the plane split in two, I had faith, she would hold out her hand and draw me to the safer part.

"Smile. Don't believe it, but I prayed to her silently over Dallas. We came down into a thick gray overcast, and it seemed that we were going to be inside it forever. I prayed to her rather than to the pilot. Isn't that crazy?"

"Yes, but interesting. Go on, George," Elaine Smith said, brushing a strand of hair from her face, and continuing with her notes.

"We landed at El Paso around sunset. The desert was filled with a cool brown light and long purple shadows, with the saguaro cactus sticking up in the sunshine. The fellow carrying my baggage wore a sombrero. Now I wasn't as frightened. I'd actually gotten to speak to her. I said: 'You've been wonderful. Will you be on the flight back tomorrow?' She smiled: 'Yes, sir, I will.'

"I'll have to admit that before the flight I thought of debauchery in Juarez. Drinking and sex. A great dark fierce woman. . . . Well, when I went downtown from Sylvia's (which, by the way, is a very nice place in a beautiful part of town) I was very depressed. You know, divorce is basically saddening, if you think about it. I imagined how lonely Mary must be, just out of the sanatorium, by herself with Davey at the inn, explaining: 'No, Daddy won't be living with us,' and all that. I even had the passing idea of phoning her—calling off the divorce and flying home. Sometimes you wish . . .

"I walked down the street. It's full of pinwheeling neon signs. I'm speaking of the tourist-trap part. Past all those liquor stores, past a dozen bars with the swinging doors, not even wanting a drink. They have big, high sidewalks, and I kept stumbling. I'd pretend to be looking in the windows of the curio shops, at the racks of turquoise rings, and the sombreros, shawls, and silver candlesticks, wanting nothing, wishing I had gone to bed. There was a lot of rock 'n' roll around, mixed up with the mariachis' singing, the Beatles and the Rolling Stones, and a lot of whooping and yelling from the bars. Some American college boys, I guessed.

"I went down a side street, miserably depressed and lonely. Believe me, if you ever get divorced, Tor, don't leave Sylvia's—"

"It's not likely," drawled Torvald Smith, fondling his wife's hair, and almost simpering, George thought.

"Now people began sneaking up to me out of the dark. The voices had only one message: 'Pussy! Pussy, señor!' At first I was polite, trying to explain to them: 'No, thank you. Any other time I'd be glad to, but I'm getting a divorce, and—' 'A French girl, señor?' 'No, no thank you.' 'A French girl and a dog?' 'Oh God, no. Please!' 'Pussy, sor?' 'No, I'm afraid not. I'm getting a divorce . . .'

"It went on like that, and I ran into a bar. I went to the men's room, and when I came back there were the cards of three houses with girls' names listed slipped under my beer glass. Down the street again, and they were after me. Do you think it was a game by now, Tor? I bought a turquoise green dress with lace borders, for my stewardess. I spoke to her in my thoughts now just as I had on the plane, as if she could protect me from debauchery as she had from the crash. Wrapping the package, the nice young man in the store asked: 'Señor, do you want some pussy?' It was the most abysmally depressing night of my life, Tor!"

"Well . . ." Torvald Smith frowned, looking up from his yellow-page draft. "Did you finally get any pussy, or what?"

"God, no! How can you ask? That's what I've been trying to—"

"Pussy is pussy, and you can't be fussy."

It was advice a cab driver had given them many years ago, and they both laughed.

"But seriously," George Pectin said. "The whole business is frightening. Because nothing happens. Divorce is such a cut-and-dried affair done this way. A document typed by clerks, a visit to the judge's chambers, and there you are. I sort of wished for a ceremony. Señor Vegas came to the waiting room with a paper, and said: 'Mr. Pectin, your divorce will be valid tomorrow.' I said: 'It will? Isn't there anything more?' 'No, nothing.' I walked out in a complete daze, feeling that nothing, and at the same time everything, had happened, blinking in the sun. I walked around for a bit, and got my liquor. There didn't seem any point in buying souvenirs, and I did have my gift for her. A truck pulled up beside me. Two men got out, and they were carrying an enormous wedding cake—"

"Pectin . . ." Elaine Smith was looking at her watch.

"Just a little more. She was there at the airport. Just as she promised, and happy to see me. While boarding I murmured in her ear: 'I have something for you!' and tapped the package in which I was carrying the dress to go with her red hair and green eyes. We flew off, and I could hardly wait to talk to her, but she was busy, and the captain announced over the intercom that we might encounter some rough weather near Dallas.

"Strangely enough, my worries about the crash hadn't come back. I could talk about them freely, and did, to the man sitting next to me. I even laughed to him about the possibility of a crash. He was a lawyer, I think. I said, as the plane trembled and black scud clouds flew past the windows: 'You see what feeling guilty can do. Because of guilt, in the fine weather coming out, I was in terror. Now in dangerous weather, I have no fear at all.'

"This man looked at me. He had a long nose and his eyes were like needles. He said: 'You didn't feel guilty for the way you treated your wife. You didn't feel anything.' 'What?' I said. 'That's outrageous. I know what I felt!' 'You felt guilty for *not* feeling guilty,' he said, penetrating me with his little eyes. 'That's all you cared about.' 'Not true!' I yelled at him, and the 'Fasten Seat Belts' warning was on. The lights were flickering, and I heard a pile of silverware crash in the stewardesses' cabinet.

"My neighbor was yelling at me again He said: 'How dare you include the rest of us in your dream?' He meant about crashing. I had to admit he was right. I mean, even if *I* have committed a sin, that doesn't mean it would be aesthetically pleasing to God to have other people in the plane suffer for my wrongdoing."

Torvald Smith closed his eyes, and yawned. His wife said: "We have a deadline, Pectin."

"Almost finished. We flew into a really terrific storm over Dallas. The thunderheads must have reached up to forty thousand feet, and they were all around us. It was black outside our windows, with terrible lightning flashes, and the plane was hitting walls of air and dropping into pockets. The passengers were calling out, and I saw my stewardess helping them. I thought again: 'She's here, and it will be all right,' and I must admit that I communicated to her via a sort of prayer: 'I bless you, and love you. . . .' Well, never mind. But one thing did amuse me. I caught a look at my old seatmate, Needle Eyes, and he was staring at me in a fearful, superstitious way, and I realized that my dream *had* possessed him, and that he now wished he hadn't been so frank with me. I shouted to him: 'Well, do you want me to pray for *you?*' and he answered: 'Yes! Please! Go ahead!'

"Suddenly I heard the man across the aisle groaning, and he was twisting in agony. Evidently it was a heart attack, because my stewardess came and immediately applied the oxygen mask to his mouth, hardly able to keep her own balance as our cabin with the flickering lights was tossing all over the sky.

"I watched her and had a strange vision. She had a sweet but quite sinister little smile on her pretty face as she clasped him in back of the neck and fed him oxygen. She was like a criminal caught in an act of mercy. There was something furtive about her, as if, under other circumstances, she might just as well have been stifling this man. More than ever, I loved the whole idea of her. Now some other passengers were calling out. She looked around, for the first time not being able to cope with the situation—and I volunteered!" George Pectin said, as if he were still amazed at what he had done. "I unstrapped my belt and crossed the aisle, and reached out for the mask and held it to his face, freeing her to help the others."

Torvald and Elaine Smith got up together, and started toward the typewriter. George Pectin followed them.

"We got down all right, without any more trouble. The storm passed. Later on when we were close to New York, my stewardess thanked me. I tried to talk with her, but she was in a hurry. I could see that something had distracted her. I spoke to her again, whispering that I had a present.

"Landing at Kennedy, the captain turned on the intercom and expressed regret for the rough time we'd had over Dallas. Then I noticed that the stewardesses were giggling among themselves. My red-headed one spoke to the passengers, asking that we not get up out of our seats until the aircraft came to a stop, and all that business. Then she said: 'Ladies and gentlemen, this is my last flight with you because [giggle] I'm getting married next week!'

"We all applauded, of course.

" 'Thank you very much for making my last trip so . . .' She giggled and said: 'Oh, yes, it was wonderful having you aboard. *Please* fly with us again!' "

"What are you going to do now, George?" Torvald Smith asked, rearranging his papers.

"She wasn't for me anyway," George Pectin said. "I realize that. Decent love isn't for me."

"What are you going to make of yourself, Pectin? Now that you have your freedom. Isn't that the question, eh?" Elaine Smith said.

The cool couple looked at him.

"I'm doomed. There's only one kind of person I want. You know who she is."

"George, I'd like to remind you of something," said Pectin's oldest friend, Torvald Smith. He rolled a white sheet, carbon, and onion skin into his typewriter. Frowning, he accepted the yellow pages his wife had edited. *"You're forty-three years old."*

"I know, I know," George Pectin stammered. "Forgive me for bothering—"

"It's not a question of bothering. *You're forty-three years old.*"

Elaine Smith said delicately: "Time is short, Pectin."

While he waited for the elevator, Smith's terrible typewriter began clattering on the terrace.

« *15* »

An End to Shabbiness

"A GOOD STORY, George," the managing editor said in the elevator. "It took a while, I must say. We almost thought we'd have to go to bed without you. Lucky we didn't. . . . 'Life on Other Worlds' has been done a lot, but you made it new, fresh, easy to read."

Then why not give me a by-line, George Pectin answered, but not aloud.

"Thank you," he smiled. "I guess I ought to know how to do it by now."

"That's not quite true," the other man said. "In my opinion, there's no such thing as having a lock on our kind of reportage. Some people lose the knack of it overnight, for a variety of reasons. But you've been around a long time. . . ."

"Yes," George Pectin said.

"You prove my point. Such talent as each of us may have is never owned. It's leased, and we have to keep on renewing it. You've known that, perhaps instinctively. You've worked hard and turned it out. All right, you're no Tom Wolfe. You're not Dick Schaap or Jimmy Breslin. But the quality of your stuff has always been even. You can write an English sentence. You care, and until recently you've always gotten your stories in on time. I wouldn't want that to change."

He was a jovial man. His head shot up out of his high collar like a bullet, and cheerfully looked around. He was famous for radiating cheer even when he fired a man, somehow making the disaster seem a moment of opportunity.

They walked across the huge blank lobby. Their footsteps echoed, and so did the managing editor's voice.

"Are you all right, George? Any personal problems?"

"Well, I'm just back from Juarez."

"Oh ho!" The other man stopped, examining his staff reporter humorously. "The usual reason?"

"Yes."

"Sometimes there's an emotional backlash. But you won't let that affect your work. I'm sure not."

They walked amid great flowering sprays from many

fountains. Long green boxes in the plaza were filled with tulips, and ladies with brightly colored shopping bags bathed in the sun.

The managing editor waited for a taxi. "I'm glad it's only a divorce," he sighed. "To tell you the truth, I thought you might be writing a book. That happens so frequently with pros in your age bracket. You can almost predict it, like a menopause thing. They forget who they are."

He put out his arm, warning George Pectin back to the curb.

"Life is all in knowing who you are. If a man forgets, or indulges in romanticism, he can exhaust himself pursuing a false image. Everybody can't be Hemingway. Everybody can't be T. S. Eliot. It's as simple as that."

The novel George Pectin had never finished was about a shabby person with no sense of beauty. This man was dogged by shabbiness, against his will created it, gravitated toward it, and was surrounded by it. Flowers all but wilted in his presence. He hated his condition, but, it seemed, was powerless to change it.

This man lived in a rooming house. He heard the slop of the bucket as the cleaning woman toiled upstairs. He was the kind of man who, with Central Park a block away, knowing the Japanese cherry trees were in blossom, wouldn't make the effort to go look at them; who could see the Metropolitan Museum of Art from his window, and never bothered to go in.

This character half-created by George Pectin lived next

(*147*

door to a somber woman who had spoken to him only once, and that time to say: "I mind my own business," and slink into her room. Across the hall was a postal clerk to whom the superintendent chuckled: "Someday you'll retire. Then what are you going to do? Sit around and read the newspapers?" Upstairs the drunken legal secretary cried all weekend long and overturned her furniture. Above her the unemployed reserve officer pounded on the floor, demanding quiet, and the Puerto Rican whose subdued bongos provided the only touch of exuberance in the entire brownstone was asked to leave. Because all beauty had been given up in this place. There was no suggestion of a flower or plant, or pictures on the wall, or even artificial flowers in the dark front hallway.

Through the character he had half-built, George Pectin mused on the nature of beauty and some men's alienation from it. A curious thing was that the man in these shabby circumstances didn't have to be there. He could afford better. But a weariness he didn't understand kept him boxed into old rooming houses. His room was clean enough and light, but barren. Since leaving the house of his childhood, he had never lived where he lived. It was never good enough; he knew he would soon move on, so he had few possessions and refused to make a home.

This man, George knew, might at least have aspired to be a poet of shabbiness, historian, confessor of the small ambition, connoisseur of self-defeat, and in getting it all down might have risen above his condition. But could shabbiness understand its own nature? The shabby man had his excuses ready. Ordinariness dulled anything he did. His dreams became boring, and he wrote paragraphs of shabby prose.

GEORGE PECTIN LOOKED OUT the window. The sky hadn't moved all day. A heavy ribbed overcast weighed on the city, and seemed to have imposed a silence in the streets. He saw a faint flick of lightning.

"GRETCHEN, I'M DIVORCED . . ."
There was a mirthful sound at the other end of the line.
"What?" he asked.
"Poor, patient Griselda!"
"Can I see you?"

« 16 »

Gretchen: The First Night

SHE KEPT HIM WAITING at the Cowardly Red
Lion, a cider and coffee house in Greenwich Village filled
with chess tables. Twisting in his chair, he watched the
door. But each time it opened more young people came in,
twenty years younger than he, laughing and holding hands.

Coffee or cider, there was no other choice. The time
and space separating him from his first cocktail of the evening grew longer and more depressing. He had forgotten
her obsessions, and how exasperating they could be.

George Pectin felt the tremendous energy and ruddiness

of youth all around him. At several nearby tables a secret was being kept from outsiders. He had an impression of small crimes going on behind his back. Lighting up in the washrooms, he supposed, boys and girls emerged with ethereal smiles, smoking Gauloises, and they moved with a sort of airy grace, giggling, among the crowded tables. He knew what they were up to, and exchanged smiles with one or two. Except for there being no liquor, he liked the place. Its atmosphere was subdued, but cool and free, especially the music. Instead of jazz these young people listened to Beethoven Quartets and selections from Hindemith.

"Here you are."

"Set up the pieces, Pectin. I'm going to beat you."

Immediately on each other's nerves:

"Gretchen, frankly, I don't care much for chess any more."

"Well, you can go home then. I want to play."

"All right, for a while."

"If you won't, I'll ask somebody . . ."

He soon found himself in a terrible bind. She played chess as she did everything else, abruptly, heedlessly. Worse, she was arrogantly determined to win, but had no talent for the game. And the more mistakes she made, the angrier she grew, and the farther away he was from his first drink. Beyond this, the hand-to-hand terms of the contest she laid down, the bravado with which she promised to teach him a lesson, were so insolent that his self-respect wouldn't let him take the easier way out and arrange a tactful defeat. He won four or five games. The sickly-sweet taste of cider made him long to replace his mouth with another, and start fresh.

Now she had exposed her queen.

"Are you sure you want to do that, Gretchen?"

"Oh, crumb!" She snatched back the king's pawn, and glared at his infiltrating white pieces. With her big arm poised over the board, her brows contracted, his date had turned into a thundercloud.

"Let's stop now."

"Play!"

"You'll lose your queen again."

She had been out in the sun. Her tanned breasts and arms quivered. Emerging from the white sleeveless blouse, they seemed more massive and powerful than ever. The density of this body, the heaviness of womanly arm and shoulder across the table, fascinated him. A desire for her, completely out of control, rose up in him. Before he knew what he had done, he clasped her brown arm. Gretchen cried: "No!" and stormed to her feet, knocking over the pieces on the chessboard. She walked away from him, and out of the Cowardly Red Lion, slamming the door behind her. George Pectin dropped dollar bills on their table and followed. He caught her as she was about to get into a taxi.

First she had to buy a bathing suit. She wanted to look nice for her father. They would be sailing on Long Island Sound tomorrow. She, her father, and someone who was supposedly going to be his third wife. "Almost my age. He makes me compete with them." She had to furl a spinnaker better than all his women.

George said: "I'll meet you in the bar across the street." In a few minutes she came in wearing a black straw cart-wheel hat.

"Do you think he'll like this?" She held up the blue bathing suit.

"I would."

"*Will he?*"

"How should I know?" George Pectin said. "Please have a drink, Gretchen, and refrain from being mean if you can. I haven't done anything to you."

She looked at him with a glint of good humor, and squeezed his hand. Two scotches later she gave him a small kiss on the cheek, but added: "You're looking hollow. You ought to get out in the sun."

"I'M NOT HUNGRY!"

"Well, we have to eat," he said. "This is a nice place. You like French food."

"Not especially."

The proprietor and his wife, M. and Mme. Saudray, smiled at Monsieur Georges, who came in once a month. At the bar their male boxer trotted over to sniff George Pectin's shoe.

"I love him!" Gretchen threw her arms around the dog's neck. "What's his name?"

"Jacques." The proprietor's wife smiled at her customers.

"I love you, Jacques!" Turning away so that her hat

blocked Pectin's view, Gretchen caressed the animal, crooning to him: "Love you, love you!"

After a while George said: "I'm here, Gretchen."

"Feel those muscles, how bunched they are. Feel here . . ." she murmured, kneading the boxer's hindquarters. "And the shoulders. Tight, powerful . . . that's the way they should be." She turned back, saying: "Do you think I was deliberately ignoring you? Well, I wasn't. I wasn't thinking of you at all."

George went to the men's room. Coming back, he was aware of the Saudrays' sympathetic smiles. Of course, he thought, she's probably said horrible things about me. But I don't care. This time I'm going to hang on and stay with her, no matter what she does.

As they followed the proprietor to their table, she said: "I don't want you, but I need somebody. Why can't you be somebody else?"

George Pectin noticed for the first time that Gretchen had taken on a new and quite disconcerting mannerism. It was to keep glancing nervously over her shoulder, as if expecting someone.

"Are you enjoying your dinner, madam?" the proprietor asked.

"Really good, isn't it?" George said of the brook trout.

"No, it's too dry."

To his horror George realized that this was directed at the chef, who stood behind M. Saudray.

154)

"And the wine tastes like fish. I don't like it. Don't you have Riesling? ..."

She surveyed the anxious faces of three men with baleful understanding.

THEY TOOK A CAB to another bar. Here she took his arm. "Don't sulk."

"Gretchen, why do you say those things?"

"Bitchiness." She gave him a hard, amused look. "Of course, I meant everything I said."

The next bar had a booming jukebox and was filled with people dancing.

She leaned against him and asked: "Why are you in hell, Pectin? Do you want me to come with you? Is that it? I might someday, when I've given up living."

He said hoarsely: "It couldn't be hell with you."

"Why do you smile only with your upper lip?" she asked. "*You have no teeth.*"

George felt a paralyzing pain in his leg.

"Tonight I think I'll just crush you between my thighs. How would you like that?"

"Waiter!" said George Pectin. "Check, please."

In the taxi she kissed him, rolling her tongue in his mouth.

SHE FLICKED THE LIGHT SWITCH ON. Her big four-poster was unmade, but Gretchen threw a coverlet over the tangle of blue sheets.

"No," she said, taking his arms from around her waist. "I shouldn't have encouraged you. It's no use, Pectin. Not now. I'm taken care of. He loves me, I think. He'll come through."

She went to the telephone and misdialed twice before getting her number.

"No calls!" She slammed down the receiver. "God, why won't he call? He *promised*. No, Pectin! Fix me a drink. . . ."

"Does it always have to be Mozart? I've listened to an eternity of passionless quintets. Can't we play Wagner . . . Gretchen . . . ?"

She had the Bible down again, and opened it up, pushing herself back and forth in the rocking chair.

" 'Be thou not far from me, O Lord: O my strength, haste thee to help me . . .' "

"Gretchen!"

" '. . . Deliver my soul from the sword, my darling from the power of the dog. Save me from the lion's mouth . . . !' "

"Oh, hell."

"*Where's my bathing suit?*"

"What?"

"Where is it?"

"Lord, I don't know. . . ." George Pectin tried to think. "In a taxi, one of those bars. . . ."

"Get it for me!"

"Gretchen, it's four o'clock in the morning. Listen—"

"I don't want to listen. I want the bathing suit. *He* always believes that things should be done just right, or not done at all. Do you understand? *You* are supposed to keep track of things. But you're not a man. It fitted me just right. It was the shade of blue he likes. He must be getting married! He said he wouldn't. . . ."

She lurched to her bed.

"I don't want to go sailing. Help me! Forgive me, don't you want a drink? Get me the bathing suit. . . . Oh, go home."

Gretchen was tearing off her dress.

"Set the clock for me. Forgive me. You're nice. I need you. No, get away! *I mean it.* Go home. Call me. . . . You're kind. Why do I have to fall in love with bastards? Well, that's it. . . ."

« 17 »

Second Night

HELL HAD TURNED INTO a Broadway table-tennis parlor. Green tables with white streaks down the middle extended across a huge loft. Above each table pools of green-shaded light centered over the little nets, and the celluloid balls rattled back and forth. The players, most of whom wore green eye shades, leaped from side to side whipping over forehand drives, stood back to chop, cunningly advanced and retreated, now driving, now chopping, and every now and then moving in for a savage kill that sent the ball ricocheting across a dozen other games to the shadows where it bounced behind a water cooler or crackled under somebody's foot.

Using penholder grips, the duelists performed sleight-of-hand maneuvers with their paddles, and moved as if choreographed in the finicky attack-defense rhythms of table tennis. Hell for George Pectin was, among other things, the *ka-pock* of ping-pong balls. He had given up the pastime mainly because of the unbearable celluloid sound. Also, curiously enough, he had given it up for the same reason he quit chess: the hellish mathematical patterns these two games introduced into his dreams. Chess nightmares maddened him with infinite combinations and possibilities; the ping-pong dream brought little pops of sound in space.

Typically, Gretchen had hit on the two games he couldn't stand. Why did she force him to ridiculous contests he didn't want, always avoiding the main one? Furthermore, at this academy all that he detested about ping-pong was multiplied a hundred, no, a thousand times. There seemed to be that many white balls streaking through the air, *ka-pock, ka-pock,* and he was trapped in an eternity of ping-pong, as he had been by chess and Mozart records. How many games? . . . All he knew was that she hadn't beaten him once, and she would not.

His eye stung with sweat. He could barely see his opponent. Her white dress was stained with the sweat of her frustration, and her brown arms glistened. Her broad forehead shone. Gretchen's hair tumbled down over her arrogant gray eyes, and she shouted: "Play!"

He served again, rocketing an ace off the back wall. She threw it back. Feminine rage shouted from across the net at the mask of determination his face had become: "Play!"

Perhaps, he thought, she means for me to smile and not take the game so seriously. He tried that, and caught a quick backhand in his teeth. The paddle fell from his sweating hand. He retrieved it, vowing again to batter through all the anger she could throw at him, and eventually be taken in her arms like the others.

"Twenty-twelve!"

"Play!"

A tall, dignified West Indian with a pointed beard approached George. He was the administrator of the center who allocated tables and time limits.

"We have a tournament going on this evening, sar," he said in a courtly tone. "Could you please ask your lady to lower her voice if she will."

"What does he want?"

"Never mind, Gretchen."

"Tell him to go away!"

"If you won't take offense, sar, there are others waiting for this table. I'm afraid your time is up."

"NIGGER!" GRETCHEN SAID in the street.

George was shocked. She never spoke that way.

A soft rain was falling. To the south Times Square steamed and smoked, and glittered in neon.

"You have no perceptiveness at all."

"What do you expect of me, Gretchen? Can I help it if he's going to get married?"

"You're completely insensitive. You don't understand anything really."

She turned from him and and shut herself up in a sidewalk telephone booth. For several minutes she talked to somebody, addressing the mouthpiece with a hovering smile. Coming out, she said: "There's a place I want to go to on Lexington Avenue."

IT WAS IN THE SIXTIES, the kind of bar George Pectin didn't like. Stepping down out of the cool rain, he wondered at people like himself who gathered in small, airless places to torture their throats with cigarettes and raw liquor.

The stools were crowded with hoarse, vulgar people. Two men hailed Gretchen. She pushed ahead without stopping to a vacant place at the far end of the bar. As she drew near, a florid young man with sandy hair stood up smiling. He took her by the shoulders and bestowed a light kiss on either cheek.

An architect, Canadian by birth, jovial and full of life, Jack Treleven his name was, and he insisted on buying a round of stingers. George accepted his reluctantly, not wanting to join the man at all. Besides, he didn't know how to drink brandy very well. It left a burning taste in his mouth, and made his heart beat fast.

He might have liked Jack Treleven, but not on an occasion like this. The architect was ruddy and forthright, friendly to George and to everyone. He seemed to have a good many friends here. The bartender made a joke behind his hand. The Canadian laughed aloud and whispered it to Gretchen. He was, George decided, friendly and yet not. Every careless movement of his hands seemed designed to show that he knew Gretchen better than any man. Also they had the same coarseness. They were getting drunk at the same rate, and laughing at the same things.

She whispered to George: "Isn't he wonderful?"

"You've known him long?"

"Years."

Possibly then, he thought, they're comrades. He smiled and tried to get in on their conversation.

"Your treat, George!" Gretchen reminded him.

"Brandy?" he asked Treleven.

"You don't mind, do you, old boy."

"Not at all."

Tapping the architect's forearm, Gretchen leaned back and inquired archly: "Treleven, what were you doing with that *baggage* the other night?"

"The very word, Gretchen! Precise as always!"

"You looked as though you were going to drag her off by the hair," she said, eying him.

"You know better than that, my dear. I'm tender. Have you forgotten? No, I finally employed persuasion." In turn the blond Canadian thrust himself back on his stool. "A little teaser, she was. I said: 'Look here, you baggage, either come home with me or have done. *Have done,*' I said, 'I'm getting too old to keep going *up* and *down* like this. . . .' "

"Did she, Jack?" someone called down from the bar.

"Oh, she saw my point, all right! . . ."

This struck George Pectin as brainless, vulgar talk. He couldn't understand how a girl as intelligent as Gretchen found so much pleasure in it. Yet she did. Her whole manner was becoming reckless, and the architect's wild humor built up along with hers. George noticed too that Gretchen and her friend shared a meaty sensuality. They had the same low center of gravity, with big sensual thighs and hips, like the dolls with heavy bottoms that, after you have pushed them over, immediately come upright. (His own center of gravity, he often felt, was in his throat.)

"Cheer-o!" Jack Treleven held aloft his stinger. Genially, as if recalling his responsibilities, he asked George Pectin: "What's up with you, my boy?"

George Pectin started talking about, of all things, his story in the magazine. In a moment he realized how boring it was, but couldn't get off it. "There is life on other worlds, more and more evidence . . ." and ". . . The Mariner pictures don't disprove . . ." Desperately not wanting to, he grew more serious. The architect turned to Gretchen incredulously.

She smiled at George Pectin, and said to the Canadian: "He's a wonderful reporter. Please get me a pack of Winston's."

When the man had gone, George said: "I'm sorry. I don't know why . . ."

"Never mind. May I tell you something."

"What?"

"I'm going home with him."

"No!"

She said gently: "Yes, I am."

"Your date is with me!"

"I know..."

He saw a line of amused faces down the bar.

"Why are you doing this!"

They confronted each other over the heaped ash trays, both strangely without anger. She shook her head slowly.

"Why!" George Pectin cried again.

She reached for his hand, but he pushed her away.

"I've always been your straight man, Gretchen!" howled the architect.

Turning about, George Pectin picked up his glass and threw it in the Canadian's face. Jack Treleven staggered back, then lunged at George, and they stumbled all over the bar. He heard shrieking and shouting, and chairs went over. Then he was being held; someone had pulled his jacket back over his shoulders. He couldn't find Gretchen. The architect was gone.

He wrenched free, and charged out of the barroom, tripping over the front step and getting up again, and saw them together on the sidewalk. They had just signaled a taxi. With a shout George rushed at the man who was taking his girl away, throwing a wild right-hand punch at him. To his amazement he felt the marvelous shock of fist on bone. It was the first time he had hit anyone since the age of fifteen. The architect leaned against a lamppost, and blood began to crawl from his nose. George Pectin went after him, and was setting himself when he felt a blow on the side of his jaw. He turned to face this assailant, and told Gretchen sadly: "No, you shouldn't do that . . ."

The architect's friends came pouring out of the bar, and his arms were pinned again. A man wearing a cap stepped up, smiling almost pleasantly, and hit him in the mouth. Gasping, George was pushed back against a wooden fence, and saw the taxi speed off into the night. When the cab had gone a silence came down on the scene. The men who had pinned and punched him seemed embarrassed, and let him go. A rouged woman with hair the color of brass came forward and pressed a handkerchief to his mouth and cheeks.

The man wearing the cap looked at himself and said unhappily: "I got blood all over me."

"*My* blood," said George Pectin. "You spilled it. It's your fault."

Somebody laughed, and they drifted back into the bar.

"Have a drink," the woman smiled.

"No, thank you."

He walked the twenty blocks to Gretchen's apartment. His heart was pounding and skipping. Rather than quieting down, the palpitations came faster. He felt weak and faint, and at the same time tremendously keyed up and vaguely triumphant. At Madison Avenue and Seventy-ninth the sidewalk in front of a new apartment building was phosphorescent and sparkled in the rain. The avenue was black and gleaming, and a black mist covered Central Park.

He came to the brownstone, and as always could tell nothing because her apartment was in the back. The buzzer wasn't answered. He telephoned, and there was no answer. His palpitations disturbed him now. He didn't want to stay up all night, but knew he wouldn't sleep anyhow until he had walked off the brandy.

He crossed all the avenues to the East River. Alone in a little park, he watched a barge move toward Hell Gate. Time went by, and he saw that a gray light had come over the city. The rain stopped. A bony little gray cat ran out from behind a garbage can, miaowed at him, and vanished. He saw a man's feet protruding from a doorway, and when he walked past forgot to look at him.

Walking home along Eighty-sixth Street, he realized that the streets were taken over by people hurrying along, either to work or home from it, carrying lunch boxes and paper bags. They had peaceful faces, and it seemed to George Pectin that they were all middle-aged or old, and that nobody joyous and young would be found on the streets at this hour.

He phoned again, and she wasn't there. So, she had gone to the man's bed this time. His clothes were sticking to him. It was going to be a stifling day. His heartbeat had steadied. There was a cracked, dry feeling in his lungs. Now that daylight had come the peaceful journeymen on the streets glanced at his bruised mouth.

« *18* »

Third Night

SHE HAD COME HOME at last. Her line was busy for ten minutes. Not that this necessarily meant a long conversation: sometimes she took the receiver off and buried it under a pillow.

George Pectin ran into the street and signaled a taxi. Traveling north on Madison Avenue, the cab rolled on soft tar. The sun had turned black, and the sky was a blister in the late afternoon. People on the sidewalk tore their collars open. George had the impression of humanity streaming under a black light.

He pushed the buzzer under her name, and when there was no answer kept on pressing it until the door mechanism responded with a chattering sound. He went inside and up one flight. Gretchen stood in the doorway naked under her dressing gown, her face tired and heavy, and said: "Pectin, what do you want? Can't you leave me alone. The air conditioning broke down. I'm so exhausted I could die."

"Did you imagine I *wouldn't* come, Gretchen, after what happened? Perhaps you don't realize it, but an incident like the one last night can destroy a man. Even you can't close the chapter just like that. And you had better stand aside, because if he's here—"

"Oh, please. I'm alone."

She let him pass, and he saw no signs of anyone having been with her.

"Naturally you went to his place and had a wonderful night together. Go ahead. Be sure to tell me."

His foe laughed. "No, I didn't sleep with him. You spoiled everything. He spent so much time threatening revenge on you that we got into a fight, and I left. Is that what you want to hear?"

"Ah," said George Pectin happily, sitting down next to the record player. "Then what?"

"I went out. To see someone." She threw herself down on the bed, with the inside of her heavy brown thigh and calf exposed as if he weren't there. "Do you think it *matters?*" she said distractedly. "God, how I need a man."

"Gretchen," George Pectin said, getting up, "I came here to tell you, I want you to know that I wasn't destroyed by last night. I wasn't even jealous. Perhaps it's because I hit him and came out of it with a little more honor, which obviously he knows, and so do you. In a strange way both of you were caught out by your own vulgarity."

"Oh, now it's the gentleman!" she jeered. "I've never known anyone as gauche and inept, with such innate lack of dignity as you."

"Nonetheless you were caught out—"

"You're pleased with that expression—"

"I also want you to know that I've never felt so confident, of you, about life in general," George Pectin said.

"That's good," his enemy yawned.

"Therefore, speaking from confidence, not whining, I would like to ask you one question. Why did you interfere, even going so far as to punch me, while I was beating him?"

Gretchen looked up at him from the bed. "Did I?" she asked with weary amusement. George Pectin's air of triumphant suffering, his long, pale countenance and swollen mouth, made her laugh: "Did I do that to you?"

"No," he said, touching his lip. "This was done by the other fellow, the one with the cap, but you're responsible."

She touched his cheek and smiled.

"I'm sorry."

"What I'm getting at is that we have a rendezvous," he

said, looking down at her. "Nothing you do from this point on can stop me."

"From what?" she asked, tired again.

"Loving you, more than I've ever loved anyone. I realize all the implications. Ours isn't the usual relationship. But in my opinion we've crossed a border together. I consider last night with all its violence a sort of communion. Do you suppose I've been thinking of anything else from the moment you two left in the cab? You know, this morning I called in sick. It's only the second time I've done that in my life. And the other time was years ago, now that I think of it, after my first evening with you. Today I've been sitting in my underwear rinsing my cut mouth. All day long I've felt a tide, like a magnetic or gravitational force, drawing me toward you. And, Gretchen, I suspect you've felt it too. If you haven't, I'll say this: it's possible that you love me, and don't know it yet."

His antagonist stared up at him with a look of anger he knew to be the other side of love. She got up and brushed past him.

"Oh, God, my head is splitting. . . ."

"I thought we might have dinner," George Pectin suggested.

Gretchen shook her head without speaking.

"I know you're tired," he went on. "I am too. Maybe slept an hour, if that. But it's only just getting dark now. Why don't we wait a little while? Re-establish the day. A bite to eat . . ."

While he was speaking she went to the refrigerator and

took out the remains of a cold-cut supper—a half-dozen pieces of baloney and liverwurst. Collecting a knife, bread, and mustard, she set the plate before him.

"May I have a beer?"

"There's nothing to drink in the house, and I don't want any," she said. "I just want to sleep."

She moved exhaustedly to the record player. Eating dry cold cuts and listening to the Mozart quintet, he felt the moment and mood slipping away, and knew that she was contriving this.

"Couldn't you play something a little warmer for once!" he cried out angrily, switching it off.

"I'm warm enough," she said. As though he were an old man or a little boy, Gretchen shrugged out of the dressing gown in front of him. She got into bed, rolling the sheet around her.

"You'll have to go home now."

He answered: "I'm going to stay."

Without moving, she asked: "Where?"

"In bed with you."

He undressed slowly, and came toward her.

"Pectin."

"Yes."

"Wait . . ."

Wearily she pulled herself up on one elbow. "I don't want you here," she said in a low voice. "Do you understand that?"

"Yes, but I don't care. I've got to be with you."

"Get in then. But remember, I'm going to *sleep*. Don't

touch me, Pectin. Don't touch me! I'm warning you. If you do, you'll be sorry."

With a lunge away from him, she turned off the light on the bed table. Feeling his way cautiously, he got into the dark bed beside her.

George Pectin fell asleep and dreamed that he was under the covers laughing and playing with the lady. She had imprisoned him, and wouldn't let him get away, and was laughing and tickling him. Sometimes they would stop and rest under the covers, her deep breaths against his quick ones, and then fight again, and he played in her embrace. Later in the dream he was terribly upset, and wanted a drink of water, and woke up.

Awake in the dark room, he heard the same soft breath close to him. He called out and clasped her. But this body thrust back from him. There was a growl, as if from the depths of a cave, and a shout in the dark. He received a violent blow on the back of the neck, and in a fury leaped to hold down the one who was attacking him.

But he could not. Big soft arms and legs slipped from him and fought. The darkness became the home of a furious woman whose only aim was to make him sorry. He bit her then, and gripped her with his legs. She caught him too, and for a moment they were locked. But this was insupportable to her, and having less leverage he was cast away, then himself trapped and all but strangled before breaking free. He felt his forces gathering and also ebbing. He was gasping and at the end of his rope, and knew if he tried all his life he could never win this struggle. He lay on his back in the stifling dark, and heard a peal of laughter.

The light was switched on. Gretchen stood by the bed with her black hair and eyes wild.

"You'll never have me, Pectin! Never!"

IN THE CHAIR AGAIN he mopped his face with a cool, moist cloth and drank the glass of milk she had brought him. Gretchen kissed his brow with mocking tenderness.

"We love each other, is that it? Do you still think so?"

Following him to the door, his enemy said: "You'll be back, won't you, Pectin?" She peered at him curiously: "Won't you?"

George Pectin went into a spasm of coughing.

"Shh! You'll wake the house!"

PART IV « *The Search* »

« *19* »

A Family Falls Apart

GEORGE PECTIN'S GRANDFATHER DIED. He suc-
cumbed angrily crying out at dawn: "No!" He did not
pass away because, after his wife's death, life held no mean-
ing for him. His life meant as much as, or more than, ever,
because he was closer to the end of it. There was nothing
else for him, and he fought all night long to stay awake.
But in spite of this devotion, and all the doctors could do,
his old heart gave out. He gasped and fought to outbreathe
his heart's failure. The terrible gasps rumbled and rattled
out of him, and his old eyes were staring wild.

When he was gone the Italian woman, Maria, flung herself on top of his warm body, "hamming it up," as his daughter, George's aunt, reported with a shudder, "disgustingly." Aunt Martha observed that as she lay on the body the housekeeper had one eye open to see what effect her theatrical grief might have on the others. Besides herself, there were three witnesses: Martha Travis; her husband, Tom; and the family physician, Dr. Sears, who had been expecting the end for weeks and marveled at the old man's stubbornness. An hour or so later Maria was seen rummaging in the linen closet.

The mystery of his passing lay perhaps in the fact that the sad event produced not the slightest mystery. His last hour offered no hope, consolation, or relief. It left everyone with a feeling of emptiness and sorrow, and a series of negatives to ponder. It wasn't possible to pretend that he died without pain. His pain at the end had been terrible. Nor could it be said that toward the end "he wanted to die." The truth was that with all the pitiful old strength of nearly ninety years he wanted to live another ninety, and at the final moment he would have bargained for ninety seconds.

It couldn't be said that at some point he murmured blessings or that a smile came to his face; he cursed his condition as long as he had the strength to do so. He was never mercifully unconscious, as his wife had been, but wildly awake to his dying. Nor could it be reported that in the end he gave up the Italian woman and became reconciled to the estranged members of his family. In cold fact he was reconciled to nothing, and gave up nothing and nobody, including Maria, and relinquished no part of the life he was being forced to leave without his consent.

At the funeral Maria was denied a place in the family pew. She cried three pews back. Her sorrow appeared genuine enough; at this stage, it was pointed out, she had nothing to gain by weeping. The will revealed that the housekeeper had nothing more to expect. Of course, Aunt Kitty's insurance policy had already been signed over to her, in accordance with the old man's wish. It was determined sometime later that she had made off with a considerable supply of blankets and bed linen.

George Pectin didn't attend the funeral. When his sister Janet phoned him at the magazine to report his grandfather's death, he burst into sobs and lay face down on his typewriter keys. He refused to move from this position. The next morning he was taken to the farm.

CLAD IN HIS RED BATHROBE, George Pectin was sipping tea on a flagstone terrace. He sat in an aluminum garden chair and placed his teacup carefully on the glass-top table in front of him. About fifty men and women were enjoying tea and soft drinks under the late-afternoon sun. A few played croquet. It was the farm's social hour. Except for the detail that all the guests wore the same color robes, it might have been supposed that a fashionable lawn party was in progress. And finally, considering the caliber of the guests, this was so.

"Mail?" George smiled at the orderly. "Oh, thank you."

It was nice of Janet to keep him up with things.

He looked better than he had in years. After two weeks the dark circles were gone from under his eyes. He was thin, but his color would have been good even if he were not tanned from hours of lying in the sun. Already, he told his hosts, he had started to look forward to New York and getting back to his desk at the magazine. Yet that life he would shortly rejoin still appeared flat and remote. Manhattan was like a Japanese landscape off somewhere. He couldn't imagine the events taking place in the skyscrapers having anything to do with him. It was the same with news from Janet, and the one note he had received from Mary and his son. They seemed as unconnected with him as dry leaves. Even so he picked up Janet's latest, watched his hand open it, and read:

Dear Brother, I didn't learn for two weeks that they had taken you away. So my last must have been forwarded, and seemed quite cold to you. Well, you'll be back before long, I trust. I understand that the news of Gramps's death was what prompted your departure. I'm sorry I had to break the news directly via phone, but what else would you expect me to do? I assumed then that you were capable of standing up to life's vicissitudes.

Probably the basic problem for you, as you've mentioned before, has been a consciousness of having failed your early promise, and feeling guilty about it. At the farm, I suppose, they will teach you how to live with failure. This would presumably involve a reduction of pride. If indeed that is what they hope to accomplish, I wouldn't resist it if I were you. I mean, if awareness of having fallen short was what proved unbearable and caused you to "dissociate" . . . (Isn't that what they call it? I have an awful time keeping up with psychiatric jargon since college days) . . . why *not* reduce the sensitivity, if it can be arranged?

Well, enough about you. I thought you might be interested in what happened after the funeral. As everyone knew he would, the executor of our family estate, Uncle Kenneth, immediately put the homestead up for sale, and in a day it was bought. Since the new owner did not want our furniture, a grand auction was held. Furthermore, it was scheduled so quickly that Uncle Dougal, who was in Europe, had no opportunity to protest, and the women did nothing. So all at once our very history as a family was being liquidated. I flew to Cape Cod to salvage anything I could. They were being nice about letting us keep a small selection of mementos and objects of sentimental value before the auction started.

Can you imagine how depressing it is to see dear, familiar pieces of furniture, pictures, objects d'art, books, all the memorabilia of your childhood *tagged* and then put up for cash evaluation before a gathering of strangers? You learn that most of what you have treasured is worth next to nothing so far as other people are concerned. You find yourself on the sidelines bidding for a few of your old memories, and hoping that somebody else will bid higher and boost the prestige of what you want, even though it will cost more money. But our family trappings went for very little in comparison with their catalogue value. (Your favorite Morris chair now rests in the living room of Carpenter the druggist. He paid four dollars for it.) I prowled around and picked up the pair of decoy mallards that used to prop the front door open, and also the old wooden crow that perched on the railing of the front porch. I found a few children's books you and I loved: *Billy Whiskers, The Little Tin Soldier* . . . you can come up and read them when you get out. And—!

Do you remember on Gramps's and Laurie's fiftieth anniversary, how the family got together, we had a party, and he said tipsily that we were all part of the Scotch-Canadian mist? . . . We had presented them with a solid-gold cigarette box with our signatures copied onto it. Just before the auction I found that box in a closet. It glinted under a pile of trash and coat hangers. Nobody had bothered with it. Obviously the box had been dropped or thrown on the floor; bits of the gold had flaked off. And of course it wasn't solid gold. Dear Kenneth who had purchased the anniversary gift in Boston seems to have exaggerated the gold content, or rather, now that I recall, *let* us imagine its worth. We contributed to the plating, and should have known it. It's typical of us not to realize that for the amount of money contributed it couldn't possibly have been solid. Looking at it that way, Uncle Kenneth, the realist, may have permitted us a harmless illusion. Now that's over with. The gold box flaked, and our entire family as a family has flaked off. The house is gone. We'll all live and die separately. You're wearing a red bathrobe (even if temporarily, and gen-

teelly, in a chic establishment), and I am a "frus-
terated" (as my ten-year-old puts it) housewife, following my husband's career around from one atomic
installation to another.

All my love, Brother Dear. Let's console each
other. Come visit with us when you're well, and we'll
regale our in-laws with tales of our childhood from
a bygone era. Love, Janet.

« 20 »

Last Day at the Farm

GEORGE PECTIN WAS SUNNING HIMSELF on the terrace when the white-haired man approached shyly.

"Do you mind if we talk?" he was asked.

"No, Doctor, sit down. I guess we're due."

His stay must be nearly over, George understood. This diffident invitation signaled the end. A chat with Dr. Moses Wilson, founder and director of the farm, invariably preceded each guest's return to the world. Everybody knew that once their dialogue was joined the guest would be sure to leave, often within the hour. Those who had been most afraid of life bolted back to it after exchanging ideas with Dr. Wilson.

He was a small man with a pock-marked face and gentle smile, and wore a tweed suit and vest even on a warm June day. Dr. Wilson also carried a white plastic hearing aid which he put on during interviews and adjusted now, leaning toward George Pectin.

"Knowing your busy schedule, it was good of you to spend a few weeks with us."

"I hadn't much choice, had I?" George laughed.

"We've enjoyed having you. I hope you weren't bored though, with nothing to do. Working on a magazine like *Forecast* must be a tremendously exciting and satisfying challenge."

"No, I don't get much satisfaction out of it any more."

"I envy you," the director said, revealing two rows of small, perfectly even capped teeth.

"Please don't. It isn't necessary."

"However, it has crossed our minds . . ." The director coughed. "That, perhaps because you were bored—for a man whose specialty is communication, you haven't been very communicative. Our people say they find you polite and sometimes talkative, but not responsive, which is a different thing. Why do you suppose that would be?"

"I'm here. You're there. That's the best way to express it."

"Oh, we can do better than that," his counselor laughed.

"I despair," George Pectin said, "of getting across my point of view—that is, trying to 'explain' my presence here—because my remarks would only confirm your understanding that I am half-baked, unstable, and immature, unwilling to face life as it is, and because of this, and the passing of people dear to me, and certain other disappointments, have been asked to recuperate in tranquil surroundings. You know it already. I know it too. So what is there to talk about?"

"Being unwilling, I think you said, 'to face life as it is.'" Dr. Moses Wilson smiled. "You seem almost proud of this."

"I am indeed. Although it's not life I refuse to honor, but rather aging and death."

"*What* and death?" the director asked, adjusting his aid.

"Getting old."

"Ah hah." The doctor drew a pipe from his pocket and tapped tobacco into it. "But that's all rather part of the game, one suspects."

"I don't think so."

"We've only to think of the great cycle, of which we're only an infinitesimal part. The flowers . . . Look!"

His guest watched one of the farm workers clipping a bouquet of roses, and said: "I am not a flower. I'm a man, different from all other animals and all forms of vegetation and superior to them, claiming privileges beyond theirs. I'm not reconciled to being cut down in my season, and don't intend to be."

"Bravo! Unfortunately, we have no choice." The doctor laughed and lit his pipe.

The guest said nothing.

"You believe we *have* a choice—that in a manner as yet unexplained we can remain eternally young. Perhaps you've located a fountain of youth somewhere," Dr. Moses Wilson jested.

"I have faith that I can do something," George Pectin said to himself.

"Forgive me, Mr. Pectin. We're only chatting. Do you realize how immature your point of view is?"

"Of course. So far as I'm concerned, maturity is another word for resignation. And I don't intend to resign." George Pectin turned to the pipe-smoker into whose care he had been entrusted. "Did you ever notice something, Dr. Wilson? When a man runs amok with an ax or jumps out of a window, the newspapers practically always—I mean three out of four times—report that 'he had been under a psychiatrist's care.' Have you observed that? It's amazingly common. Check it for yourself, and then ask why. I'll tell you. It's because your method is to tame irrationality with reason, standoffishly, instead of embracing your patient and going along with his wild dream even for a little while, and seeing what would happen in *your* imagination if you entertained it."

The director nodded, drawing on his pipe. "I am in a fledgling profession. We're certainly not perfect—"

"Perfect!" said George Pectin, laughing at his counselor and guide. "In my opinion, the record is *miserable*. It seems to me that if more than one, at the most two, of a doctor's patients jumped off a roof or killed somebody, the doctor ought to be disbarred—if there *is* such a thing as psychiatric malpractice."

"On what grounds, Mr. Pectin?"

"Incompetence . . . or coldness. Lack of love."

Dr. Moses Wilson screwed up his mild, pock-marked face and offered it to the sun. "There's bound to be a certain amount of resistance," he murmured from behind his pipe.

"Are you surprised? Why wouldn't the patient resist the nagging authority of common sense?"

"No, no. I was referring to *our* resisting the *patient*."

"*Your* resisting?"

"Look at it from our point of view," the doctor said. "I mean in the mental field. As a rule, our patients aren't very nice guys. We have to deal with utterly selfish, introverted, hostile people all day long. It's most depressing, I can assure you."

"But that's your *business.* . . ."

"True," his counselor nodded. "And I for one didn't realize what I was getting into."

George Pectin took out a cigarette, and they smoked in silence. The session was taking a bad turn. We're not connecting, he thought. He felt obliged to get on friendlier terms with the white-haired little director, but the man kept putting him off.

"The general thinking of your staff, I'm sure, is that we whom you whimsically call 'guests'—which we are, I suppose, in that our stay is voluntary and paid for by various chic trusts—ought to sit out on the lawn, relax, gain new perspectives and a healthier attitude. In effect, we are to repent of the immaturity that brought us here. Repent of loneliness—"

"Oh, say, speaking of that . . . I'm sorry," the doctor interrupted in a kindly tone. "But it's also been observed that you've had no family come to visit you. Now, of course, you're divorced, but there are others. Your father and mother, I believe. Would you like to have them come over for an afternoon?"

"I would not," said George Pectin. "Quite apart from the fact that they haven't seen one another for thirty years, and probably wouldn't recognize each other . . ."

"Or your son," Dr. Moses Wilson suggested. "I'm sure your former wife wouldn't object. Have him over for the day. You know, there's a fine electric-train set in the rec hall. I'll help you put it together if you like. I used to get a great kick out of helping my boys—"

"Play with the trains."

"Yes, it's . . ."

"Somehow, Dr. Wilson, and please excuse me, I thought you would turn out to be an enthusiast of toy trains. I don't mean to be rude, I swear I don't," George Pectin said angrily, "but so far as I can determine there's no way for us to be friends. I'll say this though. You've stirred up my adrenalin. Conceivably that's part of your method. Therapy via systematic misunderstanding! Is that the secret?"

The farm director stood up, tapping out his pipe. "I'm

afraid I've upset you." He smiled. "Shall we chat again tomorrow?"

George Pectin stepped across his path. "No, let's finish now," he said into the counselor's hearing aid. "I don't know what you've done to me, but I'll be out of here before lunch. I promise you that."

THEY WALKED ALONGSIDE A BROOK stocked with rainbow trout, and paused on a dappled, grassy bank. Elm branches moved softly overhead. A crow cawed. Smoke from the director's pipe turned blue in the sunlit morning.

"I've committed some sort of crime against myself," George Pectin said. "What is it, do you think? What's wrong with me?"

He saw that Dr. Moses Wilson was gazing at him sympathetically.

"Couldn't you stay with us a little longer?" the director said. "I really think it would be best."

George Pectin said to the trees, the brook, and a Monarch butterfly in the long grass: "I'm sinking into a vortex. I want to love somebody, but can't find the ultimate person. I refuse to live, until death is proved to be impossible."

"Mr. Pectin . . ."

"I want to live forever, and be a god, and at the same time I want to be rendered helpless, humiliated, disgraced and destroyed. . . ."

"Stay with us."

"And sometimes I feel like two people. I care terribly, but also don't care. When I go into anything deeply enough I find myself in the middle of this awful indifference, which is the most frightening thing of all."

"George . . ." the director said.

". . . What's wrong with me?"

"You'll never find peace until you abandon this obsession of yours?"

"*What* obsession?"

"It would be useless for me to tell you now. You'll have to come to the realization yourself."

"I want to *know*."

"We'll explore it together. That's why I suggest—"

"Here? What do you offer? Tranquility, croquet, the scent of roses . . . No thank you."

"George . . ." The doctor laid a hand on his arm. "Ordinarily I would agree. I even employed a few little tricks to goad you back to the city. But now it's clear to me, and I think to you as well, that you're not ready to go back to New York. You'll suffer wretchedly."

"As I'm probably meant to do."

". . . Injure yourself, and possibly others."

"Then I will—"

"And needlessly."

"I'll ask people. . . . Somebody will tell me."

"You're alone—"

"And frightened," George Pectin said to the kindly, pock-marked authority. "But I'm going back. It's the only thing to do. I intend to abolish death. If I wig out, what's lost?"

"I can't stop you, but—"

"Over a carpet of immature people like me hanging on death's barbed wire, men will storm the ramparts of impossibility and become gods."

« *21* »

To the Bottom

THE FOUNTAINS OUTSIDE the *Forecast* Building sent up showers of gold. He was crossing the plaza when the managing editor stepped out from behind a rainbow.

"George! I heard you were under the weather."

"Yes," George Pectin said, as they shook hands. "I've been at the farm."

"Oh ho. For the usual reason?"

"Yes."

"Actually we knew you were having personal problems. We had hoped they wouldn't interfere with your work."

His staff reporter nodded. "I was just coming in to see you."

"How are you feeling, boy?"

"Physically, I . . ."

"You look a little thin. But your color's good."

George Pectin asked: "What's wrong with me, do you think?"

The managing editor's head came up out of his high collar, revolving as if on a turret. He smiled. "Shall I be perfectly frank?"

"Please!" the gaunt, tanned-over staff reporter said.

"You're menopausing, George. It's as simple as that. After forty, you know, we all start to get a little seedy, anxious. . . . How did that doctor describe it? The age of the three B's, baldness, bridgework, and bifocals. Do you sometimes feel hot flashes, sudden attacks of weakness, an uncontrollable desire to laugh?"

"No, I don't," George Pectin said.

"It doesn't matter. The symptoms vary. But one thing you can be sure of, they pass. You're a bit early. I haven't had mine yet. Come to think of it, if the records are accurate, I'm six months younger than you. George . . ."

"Yes?"

"You haven't experienced a sudden, almost glandular urge to write a book, or anything like that, have you?"

"No."

The managing editor waved goodbye. "Call me tomorrow, and we'll work something out!"

. . .

IN THE TELEPHONE BOOTH, George Pectin said: "It hasn't been easy. I'm walking around the city, more or less alone. I thought I might come down this weekend."

There was a silence at the other end of the line, and he repeated: "This weekend, Mary."

After a moment she answered: "Davey would love that, but couldn't you make it next week?"

"*Next?* Your voice sounds so cool, Mary."

"I don't mean it to be."

"Why not this weekend?"

"Well . . . I'm busy."

"Doing what, if I may ask?"

"I have a date."

"A date!" he said. "I don't get you. With another man?"

"Yes."

"Couldn't you postpone it?"

"Oh, no."

"You couldn't postpone it!"

"No, but I'll tell you what. I can put Davey on the train Saturday morning. He could come up and visit you."

"Mary . . ."

"Here. He wants to talk to you."

"Wait! . . ." he shouted into the mouthpiece.

"Dad!" his son replied. "Guess what. I have a new friend. . . ."

HE APPROACHED GRETCHEN'S BROWNSTONE in the late afternoon. A car was parked arrogantly in front of it, on the wrong side of the street. The station wagon with Connecticut plates intimidated him, as did the person it must belong to. It was filled with sports equipment: fishing rods and nets, life preservers, a beach ball and surfboard. He saw dungarees and yellow slickers, and a rolled-up sail, and had a feeling that someone was watching him. He backed away, and decided that he had better walk on. Draped over the middle seat, a scuba-diving suit with mask, flippers, and spear gun was turned toward him like a sentinel.

SWARMS OF TATTERED YOUNG PEOPLE moved through the night along Macdougal Street. George Pectin had walked down from Washington Square. On this hot, still evening the park had been alive with pawing, wandering drunks, clumsy karate fighters, couples nestling on the benches: blond girls with faces like dirty flower petals huddled against Negro boys with straggly beards. The old chess players were there, and delicate boys leaning against the iron fences, and the somber observers with transistor radios held to their ears. The police watched; nothing terrible was happening, yet George smelled violence in the park and was glad to be out of it.

Now on Macdougal Street he passed by beards and guitars, bare feet and sandals, flights of chattering homosexuals and lesbians, a gathering of bicycles, and black Hondas with goggled cyclists waiting at the intersections. An imitation folk-singer with shaggy hair told him the show would start in five minutes. A Negro boy with his arm around a soft blonde offered her his half-eaten fudge bar, and she bit into it. George Pectin waited at a light. Suddenly there rushed past him a strange little crew of teen-agers eyeing everybody like demented mice.

In his day they hadn't worn dark glasses in the dark. Otherwise the action in this clutter of streets seemed not too different from what he remembered. Snatches of jazz and folk-singing came out of the taverns. There was the same roar of unmuffled sports-car engines. What he remembered most clearly hadn't changed: the surging of the night crowds up and down the narrow sidewalk, the shuffling of their feet, and voices coming and going but always there. . . . As the hour grew later the tempo of the shuffling increased. He had an impression of pilgrims. Everybody on the street, including himself, was unceasingly progressing somewhere and looking for something. Yet when he stopped for a beer he noticed outside the tavern window that within moments the same faces appeared many times over. After a while he realized that the night-voyagers were circulating in a curiously formal procession.

But he was one of those actually hunting . . . for the bar hidden in the street of cobblestones. This time when he reached the general vicinity he would have his bearings. On the other side of the street there would be the florist, and next door the carriage house and leathercraft shop. At the corner of Macdougal and Bleecker he smiled passing the

San Remo, where Bill Genovese had once danced on top of the bar with two men in aprons running alongside, pursuing him.

He decided to walk east and north, and his surroundings became more familiar. He walked faster, and saw across the street the window full of hollyhocks. George Pectin ran around the corner and found himself standing in front of a bank.

It was a neat little red brick establishment, with white blinds recently painted and potted plants in the window. He turned, looking about him uncertainly. Across the street the proprietor of the florist shop, fat, bald, wearing a white sport shirt, stood in front of his flowers smoking a cigar. There was the upturned horseshoe nailed to the carriage house door. In the window of the leathercraft shop, spotlights illuminated a display of boots.

"Excuse me, wasn't there a bar where that bank is?"

The man looked at him. Taking the cigar out of his mouth, he advanced to the curb and spat in the gutter.

"Eight years ago," he said.

"It's just . . . *gone?*"

"You don't see it, do you?"

"Well, *where did they go?*"

"Who?"

"Vivian!" George Pectin said. "You must have known her."

The Greek shook his head.

"The big Negro woman . . ."

The man spat again. "That was a bum's hangout—how

should I know?" He went back into his shop.

A formation of motorcycles roared by. George Pectin walked back through their exhaust and studied the pretty little neighborhood bank. It seemed impossible that this cheerful moneychanging center could be occupying the same air space as the foul haunt that had preceded it. He could imagine fumes with a half-life of fifty years rising up through the teller's cages and drifting into the president's office.

But Vivian was famous. She couldn't simply have disappeared. Nor would the members of her court have vanished. The despairing ones with their heads buried in their arms must have found another place, and wherever that was he would find her.

"Vivian?" he asked up and down the street, and no one had any idea. He explained at the pizza parlor and the art gallery, in the record shop and in every bar: "*Vivian!* You know . . ."

"Vivian who, baby?"

In front of the San Remo, he glimpsed a tall gray-haired man inside drawing a glass of beer.

"Do you remember?" he asked this man. "One night! A lot of us. The wild boy who danced on top of your bar?"

The man thought and said: "A long time ago . . ."

". . . One jump ahead of the waiters, he leaped into the arms of a black woman!"

"Oh, sure," the man smiled. "Beer?"

"Please . . ."

"You mean Vivian."

"Yes! Can you tell me where she is now?" George Pectin leaned forward. In the bar mirror wavy glass distorted his image, making it fall around his nose and mouth.

"Now? . . ." The bartender thought aloud. "Let's see. There's a place over on Thompson Street. It's got a funny name, like a bird. The *Coney*, that's it," he affirmed. "You might find her there. Of course, I haven't seen Vivian, oh, for . . ."

"That's all right," said his customer. Leaving a dollar on the bar, he hurried out.

THE GREAT BLACK WOMAN as tall as he came out of smoke. Her bright eyes held him paralyzed as would those of a snake, and he was utterly captive. Come in, darling. Don't Be Shy. He allowed himself to be led to a place next to the jukebox. There were two shot glasses of whiskey in front of him. The machine roared in his ear. It had a thick needle, and every number was the same, a blare of sound with a thumping beat behind it. He was in the midst of a crowd of destroyed men, sodden, unshaven, bleary-eyed, spraying out hoarse witticisms, some reeling, others nodding or asleep at the tables. He coveted the black jewel on this dung heap.

Close to him, her immense bosom moved under a loose purple dress. Silver bracelets encircled her wrists, and she wore big rings.

"Please, Vivian, come away."

Somebody spilled his own liquor on him. Was the pale bartender blind? He had kept a dollar too much. George tried to make himself heard, but it was no use. Vivian was speaking to him.

"What!" he shouted. "Come away!"

At last she did, allowing him to hold her dark arms for one kiss. He pulled at her, and she followed slowly, not looking at him any more, he noticed.

"Listen! Please!" George Pectin begged against the thumping of the jukebox. "Don't you recognize me? Scared, trembling in the alley . . . You held my hand! The friend of Bill Genovese!"

She stiffened and turned from him, wandering in the darker recesses of the bar.

He followed, imploring: "Vivian, what is it?"

"How I loved that boy."

"I know, but . . ."

She kept ahead of him, circling back to the bar, and once more they were under the booming jukebox. Two whiskeys were set down again, but he didn't touch his. A man staggered between them, and had to be pushed away. The light had reappeared in Vivian's eyes. She was looking over his shoulder, and he turned to see who had attracted her attention. Near the door at a table for two sat a boy wearing a frayed army battle jacket who couldn't have been more than twenty-one. Tall and slight, trembling, he looked around, and on seeing Vivian got slowly to his feet.

She moved out from the bar, huge and dark, swaying a little, and the boy waited for her with his arms held out.

They embraced, the boy kissing her great shoulders, and the black arms gently folded him to her.

THE MAN AT THE BAR who had not been drinking buried his head in his arms. He'd had only two beers all evening. When after five minutes Vivian and the pink-cheeked boy still had not moved, he raised some sort of outcry and ran out.

« *22* »

At Muchnik's

ON THE THIRD-FLOOR LANDING he heard the guitar, then the voice chanting above. It was an invocation of some sort. Smaller voices joined in. The guitar thrummed and bucked, urging them on.

Catching his breath, he stepped over a row of milk bottles and paper bags filled with garbage, and waited on the dimly lit staircase. The song broke up with shouts of laughter that subsided into giggles. He heard thumps and more giggles. A desultory chant rose up and died, followed by a

(*203*

sweet feminine voice that seemed to come from a record player.

His first knock brought no response. He tried again, and the door was yanked open. A terrifying vision of Muchnik appeared before him, bad news poet no more but a bearded prophet. His wasn't the kind of bully-beard that Torvald Smith cultivated. Muchnik filled the doorway with an exuberant hairy holiness. A young madman two thousand years old leaped forward and butted George Pectin lightly in the chest.

"Old friend!"

"I'm not really an old friend, as you well know," said George Pectin, struggling in the prophet's embrace. "I've just come to the end of the line, that's all."

"Love us!"

"Please . . ."

The room was shadowy and hot, and filled with ivory smoke. Packs of Gauloises lay about. A young Negro boy lounged at the window with his guitar. He paid no attention to George Pectin's arrival, but continued looking out at the night. George saw the woman Mae, apparently asleep. The boy Artie with the pile of blond hair lay on a sagging couch. In the kitchen, despite the dark glasses she wore, George recognized Serena, the girl Muchnik had offered him in the White Mule, washing dishes. Two other boys were languidly playing with each other on the floor, while a catatonic girl with close-cropped black hair and a complexion as white as the kitchen wall stared at the smoke curling from her cigarette.

"Ah, Sunflower! . . ." The poet and prophet leaned close to George Pectin. "Why so thin? Your eyes!" He drew back in seemingly genuine distress. "I see terror! Violated Scot boy out of pale, Hawthorne-haunted Salem mornings . . ." Muchnik addressed everyone, declaiming: " 'And Boston's Angel cried aloud as they flew thro' the dark night'! Fleeing pale ancestors, seeking birth or death! Which will it be? Are they one and the same for him? Is love the answer, or food?" He clapped his hands, shouting to the kitchen: "Meat and drink!" Turning to George Pectin, he said courteously: "Meanwhile, old friend, dance with me."

"No, honestly," George protested, drawing away. "I'd rather not."

"Come closer then. Confess to us. Everything!"

The Negro boy struck a progression of wilting chords on his guitar. Squeamishly George realized that the languid boys on the floor had rolled to a dark corner, and were unconcernedly having sexual relations at the feet of the pale girl, who simply looked straight ahead, not ignoring them or seeing anything. The older woman Mae lay in a heap snoring. The boy with the piled-up pompadour caressed the prophet's ankle and handed him a stick. As he sipped at it, taking deep breaths, Muchnik's eyes seemed to become more fiery and ironical, and his manner more tenderly insistent.

"Confess, love, *be*, old friend!"

All at once an unbearably pure voice filled the room. It came out of the record player but so clearly that the girl with the flowing dark hair might have been somewhere in the apartment. The Negro boy accompanied her with nearly inaudible chords. George Pectin knelt by the loudspeaker.

WANDERING ABOUT THE ROOM, the dark circles under his eyes deepening into rings, George Pectin said: "She sings to her generation, but why not also to me? Why should I be locked out from what I care for? Young people think an older man was always old. They look at a youthful picture of him, and they find it unreal. Where are the lines on his face? Why isn't his hair thin? But he was just as real then as he is now. If you took a stroboscopic photograph of a man from his birth to last breath, that would show that we're all the same—only at different stages along the road.

"Why can't a man over forty ignore his years? For some reason nobody wants him to. Young people consider him a trespasser. The people of his own generation, especially all the women, consider him a fool. His longings are filed under menopause. If he cries to himself when *she* sings, they're middle-aged tears. Is that fair?" George Pectin asked.

Muchnik's bearded, burning face watched him from a dark corner, glowing now and then as he sipped in air and smoke from the stick between his fingers. Before passing it to the blond boy, he twice held out the stick to George Pectin, who blindly shook his head.

"*Essentially*, you see, I'm young. Forget the lines in my face. These circles under my eyes aren't me. Imagine cords of muscle where the loose flesh is. The fat, the sag, isn't me." George Pectin looked around for confirmation. "Watch me dance—I can frug perfectly well. There's no problem. All right, and let me tell you something else. I'm not ashamed. I know how ridiculous it may sound, but when the Beatles sang 'This Boy' they don't know it but they were singing to me. When Ringo took that walk, I almost died it was so beautiful."

The girl in dark glasses came from the kitchen, holding out a sandwich and a glass of wine. George Pectin heard a whirring of nervous chords. Muchnik was advancing slowly toward him.

But he went on: "Don't people understand that there's a difference between chronological and biological age, and the spiritual too, not to mention varying life spans. Look at Bertrand Russell. A man over forty can actually—of course, somebody pointed out, you never see a gray-haired baby. Well, that's true so far as it goes—"

With a roar the prophet leaped out of the dark at George Pectin. A wild beard and huge eyes confronted him. Hands fastened on his throat. George Pectin went over backwards with a crash. Muchnik was bellowing in his ear: "*Why don't you live!*"

The woman Mae lifted her head from the floor, shouted "Live!" and fell back again.

George pulled the thumbs away from his throat. Thrashing on the floor, he caught a glimpse of the blond boy observing the fight affectionately, and the girl waiting serenely with his sandwich and wine.

HE LAY BACK AGAINST THE WALL sobbing for breath, and then when he was better, sweating and eating, washing down the salami with Gallo zinfandel. The voice said in his ear: "Scion of Scottish chiefs, weary of time, violated—"

"No . . ."

"If not, why not?" the prophet said. "Why not be violated, old friend?"

"I . . ."

"Holy, homeopathic violation?"

"No, I . . ."

"*Be!*"

George Pectin turned away, saying: "But if it's . . . undesirable."

"Be undesirable!"

". . . out of control . . ."

"Go mad then—save yourself!" the poet said, and George felt an ancient and savage logic penetrating to the center of his being.

"Take mortal terror all the way! Escape pale, ancestral ghosts!"

George Pectin staggered to his feet. He felt a black void around him, and dared not move.

"Open the gates!"

"No!" George Pectin reached toward the owlish little

figure of the girl in the doorway. He said to the void:
"You see, I can't bear to die. . . ."

George Muchnik was laughing. "You prefer birth? It's
all right. Take Serena then."

The small girl in dark glasses came to George Pectin, it
seemed obediently, and put her arms around him. Over her
shoulder he saw that the dark catatonic girl had begun to
smile. The boys on the floor who had just made love smiled
at him, as did the prophet's boy, and the young Negro with
the guitar, and the woman Mae. For a moment George
Pectin found himself surrounded by expressionless smiles.

Then Muchnik's voice breathed close to him: "I'll help
you!" The Negro boy began to play and sing:

"*Mother*, come back to me.
I remember every little thing you used to do . . ."

Muchnik beckoned to Serena, and they went into the
kitchen. George saw the poet giving her instructions. Both
of them glanced at him while they were talking. Muchnik
vanished briefly, and came back with what appeared to be a
sugar cube and a hypodermic needle. He whispered to her,
and George thought that the girl looked apprehensive.

« *23* »

Turning On

He recognized Serena as one of those obedi-
ent New York girls who go from man to man. They ask
nothing for themselves, except to be of service to demanding men. Gravitating to the lofts of poets and painters, they
usually sleep with their masters, but sometimes, if the man
is not interested, serve only as vestals or acolytes. They
cook and do whatever cleaning seems appropriate, and are
absolute servants of the spirit. Thus, Serena served the
master Muchnik, but not full-time.

He was not her lover. She had a life apart from him,

George surmised. But when things became too difficult she came back to his place and served him until she was refreshed enough to leave. This period might last for hours or days. However long the period was, while in his service she undoubtedly obeyed Muchnik's every whim.

Now she was in the kitchen with George Pectin, commanded to help him, and obediently loving to the distressed visitor. His impression at the White Mule had been that her manner was lascivious. He could hardly imagine having thought this. At the stove, in a white blouse and gray denim skirt, she was primly efficient. It was evidently important to find a pear in the icebox. Then, waiting for the water to boil, she cheerfully set about washing glasses.

They spoke in low voices, perhaps because the rest of the apartment had gone dark.

"What are you making, Serena? Tea?"

"No, dear heart. You'll see in a minute."

George Pectin said: "I wonder if you could take off your glasses. Just for a second, so I can remember you. . . ."

Immediately she did as he asked, turning about to reveal faded blue eyes, somewhat bloodshot, and under them the beginnings of dark circles like his own. She wore no makeup. Her brow was pale and her face puffed and sleepy-looking. The almost pathetic willingness with which she submitted this pale, unmadeup countenance for his inspection made George smile and kiss her gently.

"Couldn't we go out?"

"Brill," she said cheerfully, with her dark glasses back on.

"Just wander around and talk. Not do much. That would be . . ."

"Perf," Serena answered, turning off the gas jet under the saucepan of boiling water. "We've just got to—"

"What is it that you're dissolving?"

"A present from Georgie."

"For me?" he said in alarm. "Morphine or something? I'm not going to take the needle."

She laughed. "No, dear heart. He wouldn't have anything like that around."

He watched Serena dissolve the sugar cube in a half cup of water. She divided the pear into quarter sections. Taking two of these, she filled the needle with liquid and injected into one section and the other.

"What is it? You'll have to tell me," George Pectin insisted. "One of those mushroom derivatives? Lysergic acid?"

Serena gave a small chuckle and shook her head. "Not LSD. Something new. Much better."

"He wants me to get hallucinations!" George Pectin understood. "Well, I'm not going to do it."

She drew his face down and kissed him, whispering: "It's all right."

"But how do I know?"

"Don't you trust *anybody?*" she reproved him. "Let your mouse out!"

Ashamed but fearful, he watched her inject more of the substance into the sections of the pear. The operation made him a bit queasy, and he walked to the kitchen window. A new moon drifted above the church steeple in back of Muchnik's place. He saw a group of people kissing one another on a fire escape. In the apartment a silence had fallen, broken by soft rustling sounds.

"Whatever it is," George said, "you've given me a lot more than you've given yourself."

"It's all right," she said professionally, but, he thought, with a catch in her voice.

"Excuse me, Serena. You want to help me, I know. But I also know that you're under his orders and will do practically anything he says. Just now at the window . . . my back wasn't quite turned . . . I noticed that you repeatedly and rather hurriedly injected large amounts of that fluid into the portion you're holding out to me, and put very little in yours."

"It's late! Let the mouse out!"

He took the section of pear from her and ate it, tasting nothing out of the ordinary.

In Washington Square he said: "Please stay close and hold my hand." The park was full of menacing shapes. Under the trees and along the benches they were staring at him. "I don't like it here, Serena."

"Yes, dear?"

"Let's go over to the East Village. St. Mark's Place. That way. . . ."

"Perf."

"Look!" he pointed.

The illuminated church clock had thrown up her arms in dismay.

"It's only one. I thought it was much later. Do you know who she looks like?"

"*Who?*"

"She!" He burst out laughing. "My aunt! Always waving her arms. 'Thou shalt not!' "

He doubled over with silent laughter, and Serena's hand tightened in his. "Forgive me," George Pectin said. "I'm boring. Do you know that's what I worry about more than anything else?"

On Broadway they passed by an old casino, silent and dark.

"That and being old."

"Can we trade hostages?" she asked, huddling close to him.

"Yes," he said, and put his arm around her.

"This morning I had the dooms so bad. I couldn't even make a cup of coffee. I was practically a spas! When I get like that the only place I can go except to the glue factory is Georgie's. He makes me well again."

"He seems to have that effect on people," George Pectin said.

"There isn't anybody else in the world. But, you know, I need someone."

"A man. Strong . . . not dependent," George Pectin said.

She kissed him. "We're two kids. I hate grownups, don't you?"

"Yes," he agreed happily.

"It started last night with the actor."

"Who?"

"Rafe. He's my pussy cat. But everything went wrong. First I had to make a pickup at the Slant's. I'd sent a blouse there by mistake. It came back looking like a waffle. That threw me. Then I had to forget my machine. . . ." Serena made a hollow *tock* with her tongue, and fell sideways. "Too late to go back and get it. I was bananas. Late . . . the whole thing. And of course Pussy Cat, for once, was on time. With bread! Trust Irving, you know, once a month from his mother.

" 'You're late, Serena, right?' You have to keep Pussy Cat off balance. I call him up, keep telling him I love him. He never knows whether to believe it. The other day! . . ." She went off into secret laughter. "In the morning I called him, early you know, disguising my voice: 'I represent the Committee to Save the Empire State Building. . . .' " She rocked with laughter. "You could just *see* him unwinding and shaking his head: '*Whaa?*' 'The Empire State Building. It's coming down, you know, unless—' 'Uh, Uh!' (groan) '*I can't make that* . . .' Then I broke up. Hoo, hoo. He hung up on me!"

They passed the Ukrainian church. Ahead the lights of the avenue streamed north and south. George felt a strange quivering in his legs.

" 'Give me a break, actor!' I said. Oh, I love Pussy Cat more than anyone I've ever known—except for Georgie, and tonight with you, dear heart. And Kennedy, when he died, I holed up. I was a necrophile for three days.

"I almost said: 'Pussy Cat is thirty!' I didn't dare though. You see, all this time he's supposed to be a year younger than Serena. But he's a year *older*. Danny Manganese ratted on him. Irving Rat knows, because they were in the same class. Old, old! I hate old!" cried Serena. She kissed George Pectin. "So do you, love, I know."

"Serena . . . I'm beginning to feel strange. All the lights are streaming and liquid, and the street is shining and moving like a snake!"

"Hold my hand, darling. . . ."

"I'm afraid. I don't know what I'm going to do." George Pectin shivered.

"Shh. We'll go sit in the park."

"Where?"

"In the little triangular park. See . . . where the benches are."

"I can't make it."

"Yes, we can." She guided him along the sidewalk. "It's all right. I'm feeling a little funny too. I don't think I want my shades any more." Putting the dark glasses in her blouse pocket, she went on in a singsong: "Pussy Cat is getting Mexican. 'For a non-lush,' I told him, 'you drink too fast.' 'That's all you know,' he said. Brush City! And then who should come in but that rotten drunk, Maggie Mullen. Coming on like Buster's gang. *Tock*. I had a problem. First, I did the masochistic scene. You know, moving around the table so she would have a better chance at him. But then I thought, why? So I said: 'You've got somewhere to go, Maggie, right?' But then Mr. Clean pops up. 'Serena, I despise rudeness.' The actor! You know, forget it. 'Okay, Serena. You want to home to bed, is that it?' 'Sure, Rafe.' 'Well, fine. Maggie and I will look around. Be seeing you.' Like that, alone! I had all the brandy in New York. Of course, not having my machine with me I probably saved . . . Darling, are you all right?"

How could he tell her? "I'm so hot. It's stifling. I can't breathe. . . ."

"You *can*. You're breathing *beautifully*. Sit down. Hold my hand. . . ."

"Hold me!" George Pectin murmured, trembling. He felt the darkness like a cloth in his throat.

"I love you, I love you!" she whispered, as if panic-stricken.

"I'm boring!" George Pectin cried out. "Boring! Unattractive! Nothing! Nobody!"

"Oh, *go*, dear heart. The mouse is out!"

"Boring!"

With a shudder the fear passed from him. The pretty little park was like an island. Traffic flowed all around without touching them, and it would be all right.

He turned quietly to her, and asked: "It's true though, isn't it? As a man, I'm quite ordinary."

She gave him a sleepy smile, and shook her head.

"I'm *not* ordinary?"

"Let's face it," the small, sleepy voice replied, "you're

(*217*

not Steve Stunning, but you've got something." Serena looked at him owlishly, and pronounced: "You're a secret swinger."

"I *am?* Thank you. Oh," George Pectin said, "that's a wonderful thing to say!"

He was suspended, swinging softly in the great bell of the night. Looking up, he saw a dark flower just outside the stars pressing softly down. All creation was benign under the bell and the flower, and he was its tongue.

Turning, he discovered a great rope of pearls in the sky. "Lord!" he said, catching his throat. "Oh, lord, is that where you're supposed to take me?"

"What, dearest?"

"Over the black river . . ."

"Yes, tell me . . ."

"Where Hart Crane," he said desperately, ". . . and Sonny Rollings. No, I can't—"

"Oh, honey." She saw the glittering strand. "We won't go there. It's miles away."

"Are you sure?"

"Put your arms around me."

"No," he said. Now he knew what her deceitful little face reminded him of: the stewardness in the storm over Texas, secretly capable of evil as she fed the stricken man oxygen. "Why should I trust you? *He* calculated everything we've done. You're going to report back to him, aren't you?" he accused the traitress.

"Dearest, even if I were, or if I am, what difference does it make? I'll tell him how we loved each other."

"Ah," he said, "yes."

They clasped hands in silence, watching the soft streams of traffic split past their island.

"Do you feel better now?"

George Pectin had been thinking. "They went to the bridge because they wanted to, didn't they? Like going into the wilderness. . . . I've just noticed something!" He got up, showing her. "Everything! The cars and the people . . . all our lights blend into the stars. I mean—this tree. All of us. *We're all welded together.* That Russian cosmonaut when he was in space said the sun looked welded into the sky. And look at the moon behind the church. It's perfectly obvious, Serena. You're all huddled up. There's nothing to be afraid of!"

"Oh darling, I'm not afraid. Only when you are, and I won't let you be."

"Except that dog," George Pectin muttered.

"The little dachshund? The man has him on a leash."

"Yes, but that leash can stretch," he said, retreating to the bench. "It can stretch to infinity if the dog pulls at it. Do you think he will? He's *coming closer.*"

"Just play with him, dear. He only wants to sniff."

He was swimming in his own sweat. The dog's sniffs were little explosions in the dark.

"Pat him. Look. . . . See what I'm doing. He's a beautiful, loving dog. His eyes . . . they're like emeralds."

"He looks so sad."

"No, he's very happy. He has a good master who loves him. See . . ."

"You're right," George said with relief. "Good evening, sir."

"Hi there!" the man said, passing by.

"You don't talk in the same way!" George Pectin suddenly laughed.

"What, darling?"

"You don't use that funny language any more. Have you noticed?"

They were holding hands, and started to laugh. He felt as if they would eat each other up with the wonderful joke.

The night was cooler. "Do you think I can walk?" he asked.

"You can do anything, honey."

They walked unsteadily to the edge of the park. By the time they reached the corner he felt light and free, and the shape of the flower beyond the stars seemed farther away.

"Listen!"

They exchanged delighted looks.

"Do you hear it?"

"Yes!"

"Can I dance?"

"Of course, dear love."

A sign halfway down the block proclaimed: MONTI ROCK III. Cautiously holding on to one another, with the sidewalk streaming past them, they hurried to the place where the beautiful Negro girl was gyrating behind the window.

« *24* »

Discotheque

THEY WERE IN A DARK, SCREAMING PLACE. On an upraised platform enormous electric guitars slung over the shoulders of three young men flashed under a small spot-light. Each of the musicians stood before a microphone amid a tangle of electric cords, and the walls, the floor, and the ceiling quaked from the vibration of their guitars. Off to one side, the small lion-faced drummer pounding an array of bright pots and kettles lifted the guitars and drove them ahead with a thumping, shattering beat. Periodically an electronic shriek girdled the room, as the house dancers, two girls in wall niches and a couple on a high balcony, flung themselves in and out of a progression of chords that moved from one crescendo to another.

A girl wearing long, lovely black silk stockings beckoned to him. Holding Serena by the hand, George Pectin followed the waitress through the dark, along the edge of a bobbing mass of dancers. At a table by the wall he didn't remember what he ordered, wanting only to dance. They went out on the floor, and were instantly swallowed up by the dark bodies around them and enveloped in a thudding rhythm.

For a few seconds his legs trembled, but then the beat took hold of them and enclosed him completely. He could no more not have danced, or been awkward or fallen than he could have flown. The guitars came down all together with an ear-splitting *prang*, and he felt himself lifted on a great tide of chords and flung away. Opposite him Serena's face looked like a stray piece of paper in the dark. A powerful throbbing mounted up through his legs. He felt a thousand little interior rhythms. He found a melodic line, and turned against it very slowly. She reacted as if sprung by his slow turn, spinning into him as though on a spool.

Hoarse voices cried into the microphones: "Do the Monk-yeh!" and they did, climbing imaginary walls and coming down. Turning and spinning, they alternated shimmying passages, finally coming together in one quick, passing flurry. Serena's hips flew in the dark. She seemed not to be touching the floor, following him everywhere.

They never looked at one another for more than a moment but were always together with the space between them. Once again there was a *prang,* and a shattering echo. He began to feel trapped. It would never end.

All at once sweat was pouring from him. He felt all his energies draining. He felt old and gray-faced and fat in the dark. Reaching toward Serena, he tried to tell her that they would have to stop.

Unbelievably the guitars ceased. The musicians walked away from their stand. He was gasping into her ear: "I've got to . . ." when the music came back on with a swelling boom, this time echoing from tapes. All around him dark forms were leaping. Serena had paid no attention, and there was no release from the terrible beat.

A gradually deepening glow of soft red and then green lights spread over the dance floor. It was like being inside a huge jukebox. For the first time he could see the other dancers. A pair of shoulders he knew bobbed before him, or rather an absence of shoulders; a pair of bobbing epaulets. Above them a fatuous face had become wildly alive. Where had he seen this ecstatic individual? It couldn't be but was Philip Rhodes, the editorial writer, the loud-mouthed sage of Shannon's bar, with his eyes shut, his bald head shining, his face screwed into a look of adoration, abruptly vanishing.

Serena threw herself into him. He turned and came back to the pale wafer face, and felt himself gathering strength under the soft lights. His fat, sweating weakness fell away like an outer layer of skin. He simply burst into a cool, light feeling. Without thinking about it, he took Serena back to the table. They walked lightly with a tremendous current flowing through them.

The guitarists were back again. Amid a cascade of jangling chords, George and Serena leaned into one another's arms. He felt an insistent plucking in his groin, and, thigh to thigh, shudders began to pass between them. These did not end in a jet but steadied into a flow of love passing back and forth. The pupils of Serena's eyes looked like half-dollars. He felt bathed in all her love, but oddly her attention roved and was not fixed anywhere. Her hands slipped up and down his bared arms, and his hands held her soft arms, moving up and down them. For all the current enveloping them his specific reaction was maddeningly small, like a tributary or rivulet, or a trifling share of the huge lift of energy that came up from the shivering floor. Yet the force gripped him and pressed on him. He felt an aimless devotion, and as his involuntary shudders quickened in wave after wave a voice came out of George Pectin, crying: "I'm sorry! Oh, I'm sorry!"

"PRESENTING Monti Rock, the Third!"

A thin young man ran out with his hair flying, and seized a hand microphone. His long hair fell nearly to his shoulders. He wore a ring in one ear, a ruffed shirt, a jacket with elegant cuffs, and black trousers. Commencing a slow lope around the floor, he began to shout:

"It's all right!
It's all right now!
It's all right! . . ."

The guitarists and drummer gathered behind him with a steady thrumming and pounding, held in and slowly increased, held in again but gradually building to a pause, a *prang*, a second *prang*, and then a crash of chords that propelled the singer around the floor bestowing hysteria like flowers.

"It's all right!
It's all right now!"

Laying the portable microphone on one ringside table after another, shaking it at one part of the room and then another, with the jangling guitars behind him demanding tribute, he was a sower who had seized all the energy in the room and held it like a fistful of lightning, which he threw back, insisting that it should be taken back and then returned to him.

"You know you love me, baby!
It's all right now!"

George Pectin was clutching the very blood in her arms. Serena's nails were painless pins in his arm. His trembling had quieted. He felt a small tide moving back and forth between them, pulsing a little.

A derisive hoot came from ringside, and Monti Rock sought it out.

"I'm not gay, baby—I'm just happy!"

A woman giggled and shouted something.

"Well, now don't say that, ma'am. Don't say it. Keep your cool. Don't blow it. Never lose it, baby. It's the most precious thing you have. What? What!"

The singer ran to the edge of the floor, peering into the dark where the snicker had come from.

"Look out who's that sitting next to you, man! It might be your mother!"

Laughter spread over the room, and he was off again. The guitars echoed into the microphones, and he moved into a shuffling, hitching, wild Indian dance, hair flying, wielding his own microphone now like a tomahawk, now like an instrument of benediction, now with a phallic knocking.

> "Goin' home now . . .
> It might be your mother, baby!
> Go on home now . . ."

Time fell apart. Monti was gone, and they were on the floor again. Nothing had changed. The guitars and the electronic shriek were the same. The vision came on George Pectin slowly. He became aware of eternity in the form of a great rooted thrust rising from the dance floor. Seeming both liquid and airy, it pushed up through the dancers, who were all part of it. The presence swelled up through him, and Serena like a little tossed fragment of debris was writhing in it. The guitarists stood jangling like sentinels with huge ammunition belts. The dark figures around him blended into many shapes. The darkness burst, and he began weeping and laughing because he knew that we never die, and the dance was endless.

Then the dancers opened up like the sea, and a black wheel grew among them, growing and deepening until they were no longer there. Without any appearance of spinning, it gradually drew in at the center with an ever more powerful pressure. The cave or tunnel grew toward him, and he felt a river of wind at his back carrying him toward this dark place.

An irrelevant little presence was beating about him like a moth. Lights like roses grew where the tunnel was, and people were streaming from the floor. Serena was gripping his hands and calling to him, and she led him back to their table in the shadows.

Crashing guitars brought the singer out once more, shuffling, hitching, faster and faster, thrusting out his microphone, knocking on the air with it, distributing benedictions, a screaming sower with his hair flying.

> "Goin' home now!
> Go on home now!
> Goin' home now!
> Go on home now!"

He was absolutely shrieking now, demanding everybody's hands. People were dancing in the aisles and on the tables.

> "You know you love me, baby!
> It might be your *mother*, baby!
> Go on home now! . . ."

All barriers down:

> "It's all right now
> Goin' home now
> Go on home now! . . ."

The lights began to go on and off to a roar of protest.
"Where were you last night, baby, when we needed you!"

> "Go on home now!
> Goin' home now! . . ."

« 25 »

Going Home

A STEADY WIND BLEW them like leaves along the dark avenue. Serena laughed and turned in the wind, and leaned back against it, letting it blow through her, but he was being borne on a river. Serena was a waif on the wind who would be tossed and probably left wherever it might take her, but he had yet to be born.

"Are you all right, dear heart?"

"Yes, Serena, but do you see the blackness folding around us?"

"No!" she said, frightened and moving away from him. "I don't see that. I don't want to. . . ."

He soothed her: "I'm sorry. I shouldn't have—it isn't really."

But it was. He could almost feel the petals. He took her under the shelter of his arm and comforted her, but she was not with him. He felt her struggling a little. She looked up at him with a trace of fear.

"I'm sorry," he said again, off by himself.

The wind was diminishing for Serena into small flutters. She gave her head a decisive shake, as though waking. The night river carried him unhurriedly by her side. The little moon was gone. The park was empty. Wind was flowing under the arch in Washington Square.

The room overflowed with books and record albums and toppling piles of magazines. By her bedside there was a shining golden cup and a dish filled with black olives. She lay back on the white sheets, still in the denim skirt and blouse, quivering without reference to him. He sat on the edge of the bed looking down at her.

"Serena . . ."

Far from him, she murmured: "It's all right . . ."

He started to say: "I'll never—"

"It's all right."

Groping among the olives, she took one and then another. He stroked her forehead. She pressed his hand, and moving restlessly said: "Good night, Pussy Cat."

The latch clicked behind him, and he heard the sliding

chain. He descended between grainy walls. The staircase moved under his feet like a pile of boxes.

THE NIGHT HAD TURNED RED. The taxi glided down a deep red river. Streets moved silently by, but the city around him gave off soft, crackling sounds. Red and green lights flickering on and off had moist halos. The broad current carried him past tall buildings, and he could see the moisture dripping from them. The city turned in front of him and became motionless. He heard a clearing of the throat. A small hatchet stood up against the windshield. He took papers from his wallet and dropped them into the hand that was waiting.

George shivered in the red street. There was a tremendous echoing slam. The taxi was no longer there, and he crossed to the other side.

« *26* »

Birth

HE STOLE INTO THE ENTRY of the brownstone, and pressed the buzzer several times before the door emitted two fragmentary clicks. It gave before his weight, and he went up the carpeted stairs. He found the apartment door ajar. From within a voice sighed: "It's open . . ."

He entered, turning on the switch by the door. Slowly a glowing crimson light grew under the lampshade at the far end of the room. He turned wonderingly toward this light, regarding it with an awed expression.

Gretchen moaned on the bed and turned and laughed.

She coughed and murmured: "Dear love, I knew you wouldn't marry her. . . ."

Near her hand a whisky bottle gleamed on the bed table. A cigarette was burning down to its filter with the smoke curling up from it.

"After we went swimming, you sent her away, didn't you!"

He turned back and forth between the light and the form of the woman.

"I knew you wouldn't leave me. . . ."

With growing awe, he looked at her and turned off the light.

In bed her warm thighs and arms encircled him.

"Oh, how I love you!"

Her mouth and tongue sought his.

"There never was anybody else. . . ."

He was kneeling, with his head down between her thighs. Then a tremendous pressure forced itself into her, and increased, and she cried out.

"It's all right!" he whispered.

There followed an enlarging thrust, and a cry was torn from her. Amid a terrible encircling anguish she cried out again, pushing against his shoulders. But presently her arms relaxed. With a shudder she began to draw the pain into her, laboring softly and rhythmically, and before long the man was still.

Outside the brownstone a small crowd had gathered in

the sun. A white ambulance at the curb waited behind a black Chevrolet with a medical license plate. The expectant watchers idled near a police car listening to calls crackling back and forth on the radio. The patrolman chewing gum at the wheel craned his neck. Another had emerged from the brownstone, followed by an attendant in a white uniform who wigwagged an elaborate "no" to the ambulance driver.

In the apartment an elderly man knelt between two stretchers. He took off his stethoscope and painfully got to his feet. Decades before, his face had begun to sag with patience and weariness. Making a sign to the attendants, he walked to where the pale young man was standing by the window.

"I'm sorry, I couldn't watch any more," confessed the intern in a trembling voice. "I've never seen anything like that."

"You're not likely to," his older colleague said.

"Lord! It looked as if he was trying to get born again. . . ."

The old doctor said: "He went about it the wrong way."

"Why would a man want to do such a thing?" quavered the intern. He gazed miserably into a back lot filled with clotheslines. "I still can't believe—"

"You've always managed to believe in the Virgin Birth, haven't you, Kelly?" the white-haired doctor said with a dour chuckle.

"Yes, but . . . it's strange. She looked so peaceful."

234)

"You should see him. He was smiling," one of the order- lies said, passing by.

"Please, if you don't mind." The young doctor turned away. Perspiration was standing out on his black hair like a rinse.

The older man put a hand on his shoulder.

The intern looked at the floor. "I wonder, sir. Do you suppose before we go back to work we could stop off and have a drink or something? I know it's wrong. I realize I'm immature . . ."

The old doctor picked up his satchel. "That's all right, Kelly," he said. "I'll go with you."

ABOUT THE AUTHOR

Born in Newton, Massachusetts, Alan Harrington was graduated from Harvard in 1939. He has worked for a wire service, as editor at the Republic of Indonesia Information Office in New York, and in advertising and public relations.

His first work of fiction, *The Revelations of Dr. Modesto*, a satire on conformity, has won growing recognition as one of the finest of the "black comedy" novels. Ralph Ellison has called it a "novel of ideas in which his most caustic commentary on American society, types and values is made to arise out of his most hilarious situations—a sure sign of a fully achieved comic art. For those who suspect that the American genius for trenchant comic statement has been lost, *The Revelations of Dr. Modesto* offers a most lusty denial."

Alan Harrington is also the author of *Life in the Crystal Palace*, a personal study of life in one of America's great corporations. He lives in New York City. He has a son, Stephen, seventeen, from his first marriage. Regarding *The Secret Swinger*, he says, "I am grateful to my second wife, Luba, for her help and encouragement." Mr. Harrington is now at work on a new novel and a book of nonfiction exploring means to "turn men into gods."

A NOTE ON THE TYPE

The text of this book was set on the Linotype in
Janson, a recutting made direct from type cast from
matrices long thought to have been made by the
Dutchman Anton Janson, who was a practicing type
founder in Leipzig during the years 1668–87. However it has been conclusively demonstrated that these
types are actually the work of Nicholas Kis (1650–
1702), a Hungarian, who most probably learned his
trade from the master Dutch type founder Kirk
Voskens. The type is an excellent example of the
influential and sturdy Dutch types that prevailed in
England up to the time William Caslon developed
his own incomparable designs from these Dutch faces.

Composed, printed, and bound by The Haddon
Craftsmen, Inc., Scranton, Pa.